HARD PLACES

*Also by John Fraser
and published by AESOP Modern Fiction:*

Animal Tales
Black Masks
Blue Light / Starting Over
The Case
Down from the Stars
Enterprising Women
An Illusion of Sun
The Magnificent Wurlitzer
Medusa
Military Roads
The Observatory
The Other Shore
The Red Tank
Runners
Soft Landing
The Storm
Three Beauties
Wayfaring

HARD PLACES

John Fraser

AESOP Modern Fiction
Oxford

AESOP Modern Fiction
An imprint of AESOP Publications
Martin Noble Editorial / AESOP
28 Abberbury Road, Oxford OX4 4ES, UK
www.aesopbooks.com

www.johnfraser.info

A catalogue record of this book is
available from the British Library.

ISBN: 978-0-9927588-8-2

Contents

RED SNOW

An Entertainment

'Toute pensée émet un coup de dés'
Stéphane Mallarmé,
Un coup de dés jamais n'abolira l'hasard

'O paradis cent fois retrouvé reperdu
Tes yeux sont mon Pérou ma Golconde mes Indes.'
Louis Aragon,
Les yeux d'Elsa

~ I ~

'Hold on! Hold him!'

'It's hair! I can't,' she says.

'Hold his hair. No, he's gone,' I say.

'We pitched too near the edge. It was so beautiful,' she says.

'There he sails – oh no, like a bale of something. And – red snow!' I say.

Elsa says, 'Must be something sharp. Oh dear, how terrible.'

'You let him go. Idiot. He died a hero's death.'

She says, 'He was asleep. He dreamt. Perhaps of me. He wriggled.'

'A hero's death,' I say. 'And who's to know. That accolade the last, the least, thing we can do.'

She complains, 'This stupid search. All the flowers are shut and under snow.'

'Just chance. Another year will come.'

She says, 'That's excitement for today, enough! At least there aren't people to be told.'

A flurry in the night.

'You could have grabbed him,' I say.

'By his hair? It's mad. Now, don't start on me. He chose the spot, he warmed his way right down – the void, the void!'

'Don't get upset. You rock the tent.'

'Not upset – doing my analysis, is all. Coming to terms.'

This sliding in the chill, the cold – enough!

Another scheme:

I say, 'Paradise: food and flora.' What do you think?'

She says, 'Nice for the cover. As for the book itself – you've got it wrong. Paradise is when you're dead. You must mean Eden – that's where the Fall begins.'

'There must be stuff on both. They're basic gardens. The pity is – it's Africa, that's where it starts. Besides, between the fall and death, there's just white time, just waiting for the bus. Our big idea is – immortality. Not eternity – that's over in a flash. But going on, day after day, your legs in causal chains, your head is twisting side to side and getting wiser by the hour. What we must ask is – what animals, what flowers and such you need, to live the good, the everlasting life? That's what the texts are all about, it's where the heroes come to rest when all the slaying's done.'

Elsa says, 'You're wrong. But sure – the idea's a

seller, it's commercial.'

'Not just the bible stuff – all kinds of other tales, like Gilgamesh – there's deer and pomegranates, juice of peach, manna and mushrooms. And some feisty people too.'

'It's worth another expedition. Adventures – they'll arrive for sure,' she says.

'This year the world won't end, the holes are plugged in earth and sky,' I say, 'so we'll go back, and on our watch again – casting runes, the tarot, chair arrangement, cheering up the old. Mysteries.'

She says, 'You've got the book already written. What's the point of more?'

I show her. The book, as it is. It's a block of cardboard, there's no text, just montage of an eye, a feather, mountain cave, a shoulderblade with bullet hole.

I say, 'The colour's sharp.'

Grey, yellow, indigo, a splash – vermilion in a white expanse. Could be an error. All to play for.

Here's the project, then – and no more Arctic, frozen flowers, it's off to Africa, and I say, 'We must live as heroes. Then be forgotten.'

'That's not why heroes do it.'

I insist: 'An epic. For the people. And the kids.'

She's back on her track again, her lover sliding down the slope, nearly now forgotten. She says, 'The kids? Little screwed-up guys. Too plugged-in, clued-up and clueless.'

'You may be right. But that is everything there is.'

The pole is moving, further east and south. So we follow, hoping on the way we'll eat and find a stash of something good. Fatuous, the complaining of the rigours, and the luxury.

I say, 'We've learned to look on, coldly. Then – out, into the cold.'

'Is that heroism,' she asks, uninterested in an answer. 'Guess it is.'

We inherit everything. Now, I've inherited Elsa. Ah, those ideas, the gardens, beautiful, like in the poem. Stupid! Much better than in the poem, any poem. And Elsa, my grubby muse, queen heavy with her tragedy – or, in this case, someone else's.

I say, 'Heroes need a big cast – or a big mountain. Well, I've tired of mountains. There, you don't feel free, you feel cold and breathless. Bring on the elevators. As for the extras, cast of thousands – are they willing to be turned to monkeys or to stone, trampled or boiled? Where shall we find them?'

I already have the answer.

Down at the pier our ship is ready – striding off,

then, back with the loot. Sailors – once shoremen all, their houses burned, and some throats cut – a host of ghosts a-twittering before the prow, the sea is full of them, the lifeless and the dispossessed. 'Home are the pirates, home from the sea' – but they aren't, they never are. What a fate, what a tempting, this 'going on board' – and boards these are, I stamp on them. Theatre or coffin. Urchins grown specially and sent aloft. Those sea eagles make fine weapons, if you train them right.

There's Elsa, at the prow, she points, as if she leads the ship, the breasts, the eyes, some randy sailors paint her after every trip.

'We'll find some guys to sort things out,' she says. 'Ours is no rubber raft that circles with no destination.'

'It's Nick, the manager,' I think. 'When he comes, she'll feel assured. It seems to her it's all a nonsense, floating from there to here.'

If you live beside the sea, you can never throw anything away, it all regurgitates. This whole front, this shoreline, must have been tossed in, tossed back, so many times ...

Here's a door, two halves. One half says Cruise,

the other half says Crews.

I say, 'We want to do a book. On Paradise. We hate the sea, but still I need a crew.'

The guy is silent, and I say, 'About four thousand.'

'Where you going?'

'To the interior,' I say. 'Find a safe haven.'

'Done it before?' he asks, 'This haven here's quite safe.'

'Done all, and many times before. This haven here is too beside the sea – always beginning over, as they say. For me, it's useless. I need something new. Each time a something new.'

'Food? Women?'

'I shall take my own, as much as I need – the guys you sell me, they're not dumb, they'll do as they see fit. Along the way.'

'You want insurance?'

I say, 'No – these guys aren't stupid, they know what captains are. Altimeters, shovels – those are all they need,' and I think, and do not say, 'Plus all the cash they've got,' for, sure, they are not stupid, and they know that stuff is useful, always, when you've no address, no destination.

*

Elsa does research, she knows the tricks, the history, the happenstance.

'Women, cattle, salt,' she says. 'It's all you need for happiness.'

'Is that a joke? Is that the start of something, or the end?' I ask.

She says, 'The two groups here, they had a trade – the salt exchanged for cattle, and to balance out – the women.'

'For a good trade, you need two things, not three.'

'Even with two, you need some cash. In time, it's Capital,' she says.

I say, 'If they traded women, they were really one group, not two.'

She laughs, 'That's so. That's why they fought.'

'Families, clans – they all fight,' I say.

'The guys from here, the guys from there – they didn't need accumulation – they just needed use,' she says.

'There'll have been gifts,' I say. 'And feasts. And mediators, fixers. Good beginning for a war, one reasoning's as good as any other.'

'Maybe we don't know enough to say,' she says.

'Maybe they were shorts and talls, so's you'd know.'

'Maybe the women didn't want to go,' she says.

'The cattle certainly didn't.'

'It's just destiny,' she says.

'You don't have to like it,' I say.

'That's where the priests come in,' she says.

Here's a stranger, another one. Sabrina.

'You're a real anthropologist?' I ask. 'Eating slugs? Or just chivvying guys, peaceful in their local?'

'It's great here. The primitives are hanging on, there's a hotel.'

'It'll all be booked with folks like you, like us,' I say.

'I like that "folks". It takes you back.'

Strangers into town – the gunfights aren't the worst of it.

Elsa tells me, earnestly, 'It's flown. Love, desire, affection. Isn't it funny. Odd, at least.'

'Maybe it'll fly back. You could take something,' I say.

'Why should it? Fly? Why should I? Take something? You don't mean a potion!'

I ask, 'Desire for me, or for the sleeping slider?'

'Why should things slip away, when you need to

hold them?'

Elsa. It's the eyes. They're still there.

'Precious words,' I say. 'No reason for it all. Inconvenience, perhaps, when things aren't there.'

'No, no, a benefit. A freedom.'

Here's another one! This woman sniffs out the little piece of Russia in me. How do they – we – do it, like hunting dogs? Sniff each other out, everyone is someone's game.

She's from Ukraine, she says, 'That's what it means, my place – "on the edge", "at the limit", expect the worst.'

'I guess not everyone can leave, like you. There'd be a global "tilt" effect.'

The past is heavy with her. She holds me, says, 'I'd many people, children at least, that I took care of. And they were all taken. Almost all.'

'Where'd they go?'

'They were young then, but now they're old. They would be old. Just – they never got their souls. Too young, then, and – now, they're old, too old. All the ones that's old now, that died young – no point in looking for them.'

'No, not since you must know where they are.

Bodies, at least,' I say.

'You don't follow me,' she says.

'No, I'm not there with you.'

'All those that died, they had their souls killed with them – you can't look for someone without a soul,' she says.

It's deadlock. 'Maybe you're right, and it's all true,' I say.

Elsa says, 'She means, there's been so many gone from there, they're all forgotten and grown old, and so there's nothing left, what she calls soul – it's what her parents went to church about. Candles, all those things. And if you're very young, you haven't got your soul yet. Need looking after.'

'She can't believe all that.'

'She keeps the language, some bad memories,' she says.

I tell the Ukrainian, 'I don't see you as a carer.'

'In that place, there were always kids. Trying to hook on.'

'Then the killing sprees. Why does that word, "spree" cling on, not used in any other place – why should it signify having a good time?' I ask.

'There's a symmetry, an up and down – my granddad says, they fled from times so terrible they knew those times would soon be back. He said that just before the war – the Patriotic War – they had a festival, with cannons, filled with water, shot it in the sky, and down it came! Quite out of season. Down from the clouds. Red snow,' she says.

'Anyone would remember that,' I say.

Though – she's too young, for any part of that, that history.

'It's a good thing to have inside, in your skull,' I say. 'I don't like children. They're like parcels – all that packing's quite exciting, but it's cumbersome. Then what's inside – it's usually a drag, it's broken, or too small, parts are missing ...'

'You can't like big people much,' she says.

'Not to be attached to. You look back, one person isn't worth the littlest coin.'

I say to Elsa, 'That woman has bits of me, inside. We're made like walls, the same walls, fallen down, distributed, cemented back up, crumbly bits like scraps of bread. Now, tell me – that I'm not reactionary, a reactionary.'

'That's what I think you are,' she says.

'I'm terrified of the past. I fear being made to go back there,' I say, and, 'I'm frightened of the future too.'

'That's what I mean. You can't look both ways, and you can't cover both sets of eyes. Unless you are a god, with four arms, or more,' she says.

'Why can't I?'

'You just can't. It's not allowed,' she says.

'That's what I mean, exactly.'

'Skewered by fear?' she asks.

'That's it. Kebab. Skewers – one of the ways ... The skewer does for you.'

'Think of paintings. Massage parlors. The highest pleasures,' she says.

'No cure.'

She says, 'What pathos! I don't want to know.'

I say, 'Well, that's my fear. To be sent back. The past. Not loneliness, this time, but knowing. Terrible. Knowledge.'

'I didn't think you were a tormented little guy.'

'Nothing has happened to me, it was happening to other people. Another time, I'd know how many,' I say.

'You don't think the suffering came to you as you grew up – or at least grew older – and so you have to go on, bearing everything that happened, but didn't happen to you at all?' she asks.

'Of course I think that. There's nothing else,' I say.

'There's lots of other things. You know there are.'

I say, 'Next time, I'd join the FBI. It's the safest place. You can marry there, and place your children too.'

*

We sit and chat with Sabrina. She tells us, maybe she invents for us, that here—

'A queen, Antiope, she climbed up and down her stair. She didn't labour, her stair was not a metaphor, just the way of looking out, over the walls – and all around, rich nature.'

I interrupt, I say, 'There was much more nature then.'

She goes on, 'All around, and suffering left in, and executions too, that must have resonated through the whole clan and all its servants. Yet that suffering isn't ours.'

'That's what I tell him,' says Elsa, pointing at me.

'More people lived in nature then,' I say.

'But in towns too, where you bought snuff and overcoats,' says Sabrina.

Elsa turns to me, she's angry, shouts at me, 'No, you must stop this, – this idiocy! Ignorance, the naming things, and giving weight to feelings that you've never had, and archives and the forest, the things that stay with us and stifle – yes! out of the attic we can walk! Rejoice, the trees! Look at them – and now, the blankness of the forest's gone! Rejoice, there's desert, – but it's far beyond! And here, just us, – here behind the walls: there's water, salt ... our life, stifling maybe, or open like a road. The moment! –

live in that, although it's complicated!'

I ask Sabrina, 'Whether a wind-up gramophone is closer to an elephant, than a tiger to a rat – you know the theories, about dinosaurs, they're all here, still with us, just we don't recognise—'

She says, 'We still see rats, most people never saw a tiger – and soon won't. The zoo is finished, just a cabinet of curiosities.'

Sabrina's at ease. Consuming theories, adding here a polished stone, or filing off a blip.

'My!' she says, 'this music's rich, it's cake, over the top a bit,' and on she rambles, how the Queen Antiope suffered in her life, to keep the water in the well – have her voice heard, like a true diva, with musicians in the pit, the ushers, programme sellers, all their futures, open and empty, made of glass. Or stone, glued into asphalt. All gone. Now, all gone. Antiope too. The water sinking till the well was dry, only her voice can still be heard ...

Sabrina's whole tale, so brilliantly told and musicked, music in our heads, her voice a silver trumpet – louder than the guys here in the bar – though these can sing and strum and pound a storm, like donkeys braying as they fall from heights ... And now, all over, gone, a liberation for the rest of us.

'Well,' I say to Sabrina, 'you certainly can spin a tale,'

Elsa lies, and says, 'Yes, thanks so much.'

I think, 'It means – here's the music, the tale, it's going on and on, without the people, like a city bombed but still supreme, the finest buildings stand, and those destroyed leave panoramas, futures laid open. The music stays, we go. They all go. Where to? Just glass or stone. Antiope – holding it together, an opera, surveying everything – until the well is dry ... and then? More music? Telling stories? Something new? That comes and changes everything, fresh, abundant?'

Sabrina says, 'We mustn't be too formal. Everything goes in and out, in stories, legends – it's like cats, it's whims, not plans. And like some cats, the stories don't come back – out there, alone, they have their end, their bad half hour.'

Elsa says, 'That singer by the bar – I know him – he parked his Lada on my foot.'

I've no patience, say, 'They're just country lads.'

Sabrina ignores me, says, 'My training was in systems – I can transplant livers, write music – but it's hard to deal with this – this stasis, before the transformation.'

'The fires are burning everywhere,' I say. 'The good stuff was all carried off, much earlier.'

Sabrina says, 'I hear you've got four thousand guys – a lot for such a little place.'

I'm proud, I say, 'When we're gone it'll make it even smaller,' but I don't go on, nor trust her – she is the song and not the singer, some tricky scheme that she's not owning to, those tales of queens and water in the well. And counting up resources. I'm not fooled, not fooled at all.

Later I say to Elsa, 'You could have saved him.'

'It was the hair. And half thoughts.'

'Not caring to the end. Better that way?' I ask.

'The moment. The most complicated time there is,' she says.

Fresh water here. I say, 'It mustn't just be still, this water. It must reflect. The blue above, the fish like learned angels, mute and wise. Reflecting, so's you too reflect: the water and the sky – they frame the in-between, the trees, the shade for rest, and more reflection.'

'Fruit too,' says Elsa.

'I wouldn't count on that,' I say.

'And selling.'

'Nor that either,' I say, and once more, 'You could have grabbed him.'

'It wasn't a grabbing relationship. Anyway, it was me who lost,' she says.

'He lost more than just a bunkie.'

'Get lost yourself. You – second best!'

'I want to get out of here,' I say.

She says, 'They want the tax. Women and children extra, sheep and goats double.'

'I want out. I won't pay a bodyguard. They're cops.'

'The guys say, if a big ship comes, they'll go to Italy,' she says.

'They're better off in the desert,' I say. 'With our project, whatever it turns up.'

Some good person always seeks you out. And stays, and waits for you to pay them. Here's my good person, guide and all the rest, Saleh.

Saleh says, 'Why we're waiting?'

'It's adventure, science. You must look before you find, unless it's catastrophe.'

'We need stuff,' he says.

I say, 'You've set up stalls. What more can you need? Everything for your comfort – the market, it's all you ...'

'We need ...' and here's his list. 'Shovels for the dead. Sharp knives for sheep and goats. And lots of party stuff, for feasts and victories. Not to mention pay.'

'Can't pay till we get our permits,' I say.

'Pay up. It's only natural.'

I think, 'If a little ship comes, I'll get on it.'

He reads me, says, 'It's you wanted an army. You could train us while we're waiting.'

Sabrina, on her telephone: '....hit her with his automobile. She was half Japanese. Wanted to get the boyfriend, but she would do, if he couldn't have her, and he was so offended ... no, no – no other deal. I'm not crossing you. Some drugs in it, no doubt, nothing to do with ... just neighbourhood. Tried one of those flash ransoms – a shed somewhere, all quiet till the guys get home from work or wherever they say they've been ... go down real deep for that, long time no see, no hear, no speak, haha. Not identification, never said that, identity, identity, gotta have lots of those, and now we can, we must! Bend before the wind, and nothing less than six figures – sorry, you're right, six zeros, and that's all he gets, zero, six times or more ... yeah, only numbers he'll see is on the number plates he gets to make! Haha. Tricky path, get the right card, keep out of jail. See you right, and soon: see you soon you sad old flicker—'

'That's poetry!' I interrupt. 'Old friend?'

'Old friend,' she says.

'You'd quite another tone,' I say.

'Like I said,' she says, 'this anthropology, it's all leached in to everything, drip and blur. There's no bottom any more. Or – maybe there is a bottom, and it's full of guys, and when you touch you give a kick and rise above it, above them – the creeps. I mean, that bottom, you don't want to stay on it, so you think big and biggest, maybe some thought will stick and make your fortune.'

I think of Queeen Antiope, and I say, 'Dawn here is still a wonder.'

Sabrina seems to think of stairs, narrow and white, climb to the roof, here's the moment, prayer, the pink light, three kinds of fig, someone secret who you love, body and skin, you touch all over, and yours ... will end bad, destiny again, the stairs to nowhere, water flat and sullen in the well.

I say, 'Just look at that waterwheel!'

It took the water from the lower basin to the courtyard, for the ablutions, now it's drooped, askew, slats not even stolen, pointing off like fingers, nowhere.

'Someone should fix that,' I say.

She points, 'There! That's where they keep the sacred books.'

'It meant something, then, when you got the contract – a thousand tiles, each with a different thought: "Buy beasts! And lots of charity, and die at thirty and be glad!" But then you were the boss, women and kids to show. What's it all mean,' I ask her, 'Learning by heart when you've got a telephone that's got it all inside?'

'How should I know. It's just beautiful. The view.' She waves a hand.

I hadn't seen before – her skin is mottled. The mystery comes out, all over, brown patches on her. Her story is her skin.

'It's up to you,' Elsa says, 'you'll lead those people out, out of this abandoned land. They'll find ...'

'It's these goddam permits. Wait around, and smart guys come, they're like Sabrina, bring you fear of fingers getting broken, you'd rather settle for a room and welfare, palace on an island, being a living god, who knows, you have to take the last card, rule is rule. Though – we're nowhere near that yet,' I say.

'Can't make provision now,' she says.

'I can't pay them till we move,' I say.

'You can't move without a permit.'

'I can't pay for the permit till we get the permit to move,' I say.

'Then you'll get the money to pay the guys?'

'Lots of it. Sure,' I say.

'You see,' she says cheerfully, 'You're quite a boss, with all that—'

'Everyone's a boss now. Unless you are, you're animal feed,' I tell her.

'Even start a coup somewhere, with all those—' she says.

'Can't start anything without a permit,' I say.

Later, I say to Elsa, 'If we tax the guys, we'll get the permit, and we'll move.'

'But you can't pay them.'

'If they've paid the tax, they're in the scheme,' I say. 'Stockholders, that's what they're called.'

'It seems wrong, I don't know why.'

I tell her, 'It's you, it's being bourgeois. Rise above. Life is made of many paths that lead to different places, some don't lead anywhere at all.'

'Maybe you're right. Hmm. Life is just paths. Right, but not so nice – and that refers to you.' She thinks awhile and says, 'And I'm not bourgeois.'

'You all are. I'm not. I'm science and adventure, finding out the hidden things, the non-existent, even.'

'Under the sand, the soil? Like archaeology, or digging up some plants,' and now she's laughing.

I say, seriously, 'I'll even dig, if necessary.'

I tell her, 'I'm a Bolshevik.'

'What's he – a religion?' she asks.

'Those guys, the ones that write the scripts round here,' I wave my hands around, 'They're everywhere, reborn! Digging up the old, dead things! Nationality! Imagine! Nations! Religion! All the old stuff, forced into new clothes. Skeletons, dug up and dusted.'

'I don't follow you, you're going nowhere,' Elsa says.

'Russia. You won't remember – we had a purification, cleansing – then collapse, and then more tanks and then the gas, the bombs, the little massacres, elections, parliaments, and other kinds of gas and bombs that don't explode, and then the bosses come and sort it out. And first there's talk in every street and people come out from their dens, and time goes on and hands out little pills of history, and then it's fear and wars, you scuttle back ...'

'This is Russia? Your family?'

'That family has disappeared, into the flood. Lots of money, lots of power, and spending both on tat and stuff that fell to bits, you couldn't even sell. All secondhand, like Rolexes without the works. And so we're back – they're back – to sucking up to bosses, scraping to them, bowing to scrabbled lives. It isn't hard to see. Now there's just "*intelligenty*", pure ones, the saints. Write it all down and wring your hands. Not stasis, nor transition. It is "going back". Only the pure ones know.'

'But you don't seem pure,' she says.

'No. I'm a Bolshevik. I push, it rocks, it falls, and I'm on top – away with all the rubbish, clean it all out, your boots get filthy, but your head, it's clear.'

'I'm amazed,' she says.

'That's right! Throw off your chains. It's quite a shock.'

'I'm free,' she says.

'You're stuck here, along with me. You can't have everything – but nearly everything. You'll see! We'll be on the move, these guys ...'

I'm not so sure about these guys.

The fleet out there – it could have fought at Salamis. Might fight there again.

The prows, dark as crows' bills, the sails, should be snow-white, but they're rusty and indigo. Just floating rubbish, bearing away the Sons of Africa – anything to get away. Escaping one set of cops, to proudly sail towards another.

Seals lying there like slugs. Is that a poet, with a flask of wine? Song of the Sea? Those prows of silver and of bronze – will that time return? It never does, it can't. Song of the Sea, though – that's always possible, the song; you see a dapper chap, white suit – the little boys shout 'Ice cream' after him, that's what they wore, the ones that came from Naples, bearing *pistacchio* and *cocco,* the snow-white suits.

That guy, over there, could be the poet, chatting up the lads, ready for anything, anything for sale – for rent.

All is for rent here, nothing's sold, so no resurrction, even the prayers, the washing – out of order, unavailing. The names of God you can't remember more than ten, who cares, it's better not, doesn't do you good, nor bad. Sons of Africa! how much to get away, depends how bad you want to leave. The sea! Doesn't belong here, but it's all there is.

I say to Elsa, 'I used to watch the crabs – at midnight, sidling up the beach. Precise, as if they'd all been in the cinema, and all turned out at once, and then a noise of claws on sand. Straight up the beach, into the garbage, big black sacks. The tearing, then – no sound. Just finding other crabs. The skeletons.'

'But those four thousand guys. The sheep, the goats. And chickens too, and women, children, all you need. Where'd you take them, what's the epic?'

'I told you, thought I'd make it clear. We couldn't

get the permit. The big guys don't want to let them go, but don't want them here. Put them in jail, but what's the use? Beat them up, but what's the pleasure? So, put a fence around them, and they'll find some things to sell, to trade. Even themselves. It's called "administrative custody", so no stuff of trials or guilt. The point is,' and I reach out a point and hope she grasps it, 'The trial is: being here, until they leave and get to rampage somewhere. There's no guilt.'

'Where will they, will we, be going?' she asks.

'How can I know. Can't shake them off, these guys. Can't shake you off, Elsa, unless a better offer comes.'

'What a crap story. Quite a let-down. No revolution. Sons of Africa – a spoof,' she says.

'You must be patient. It's like red snow, it doesn't come at once, and when it does, it takes so many different forms ...' I say. 'Those old countries, those "nations" – and I laugh, 'They're so scared. Just breathe "Sons of Africa" and if they don't think it's some pop group, they pee themselves with apprehension.'

'But you come from a nation,' Elsa says. 'You don't seem very clear on politics.'

I say, 'It's not the wanting to be rich – it's being rich and famous. Or just famous. The old guys, the European guys, the rich ones – all they know is trash, they buy trash and they sell it. That is all they know.

They get afraid of some guy – maybe all he knows is sand and rocking to and fro and learning things by rote, and coveting a bicycle and praying to the East. But – the thought occurs – maybe what he knows is not all trash. Maybe it isn't worth a spit or means a thing – and maybe these guys are just ignorant, or up for sale. But it's there, the resurrection. Even if it's all a con.' I turn away. 'It all turns into trash.'

Elsa says, 'You're quite eloquent. You should have had a group.'

'I tell you, it's not about football.'

She asks – she's quite disturbed, 'Where'd you get your polish, then?'

'Oxford, Cambridge, Harvard. Those kinds.'

'What did you get there?'

'You should ask – what did you give? I gave them ideas, opinions, all for free. I always do that, wherever I am.'

'Your father – did he buy them buildings, that kind?'

'They already had buildings. Did I want I give them mud huts – that's what they think our revolution brought us.'

'Sense of loss there,' she says.

'We were on the way to paradise. Now everyone's to start all over.'

'So that's where you get the fruit, the flowers, the Eden stuff. And here, in Africa?'

'Eden was a start, and people started here, in Africa. Until they found a boat that went to Germany,' and together we laugh.

The planes fly over, necks outstretched like Canada geese, not looking down, not looking at the tails and feet in front, the tiny brains don't see the flattened mountains, corrugating seas, the fig-trees. No perspective, just a destination. That's how we should be, I think.

The port resounds to sirens, but the little boats just bustle in and out, they make their own, their little sucking sound, but still the sirens call, the calls to danger or enjoyment – the rocks, the sand bars, everywhere the warning.

Overlooks the town, an empty palace, structure not looted, not yet carried off – although the inside's bare. The fort around – a pentagon, artillery the highest mathematical art. It never fell to arms, impervious to cannonades, each wall protects another, there's no void, nor habitation, just terra cotta facing on the soil heaped up, impenetrable. A fortress made for wearing like a jewel, for bargaining, seduction, not for sale.

This place must have a history. You know your

history if you suffer it. And then you are insufferable. You are responsible for everything – but there's nothing saying that you are. You bear the burden, they say you can slide out from under it – that's the choice, and no one thinks about it but yourself.

Where the crabs go sidling up, you can see the yellow city lights, as soft as butter. In walled gardens, generators, pulsing along like jaguars relaxing on the boughs: and little bars, long and narrow, shoe boxes for a single shoe. Here is every game and every risk – trictrac and knucklebones, billiards where the balls are pocketed, billiards where they bounce, a game with matches – dominoes and shells, stones and figurines, in one bar three lusty witches hoot with delight, here's another where the beggars stack their crutches, game away the night.

I ask, 'Can I drink here?'

'Easy to play and hard to win,' and here's a stack of bottles, all the way from Cluj.

We play all night, drink that dark beer that makes us mad with thirst, and then there's aniseed with extra sugar, red stuff in dirty bottles, like it's been banned, and more and more, and higher losses – written down in scripts that look like horses lying down and kicking up their legs – a meadow somewhere, tall grass and little ponds ... and at the end it's added up, the loss, sealed with a puff of gold. And given to me.

'I can't pay this.'

'Then you're ours,' they say.

'I've no intention ...'

'Absolute responsibility, remember, and no external rules,' they say again.

'I'm what I am,' I say.

'Then you may lose the lot.'

'These dominoes – the spots are all worn off,' I say.

'You're not challenging destiny, I hope?'

'That game with cards – the "lost imam" they call it ... someone fiddling there,' I say.

'You're not challenging fortune, I hope?'

'If I'm yours, what might that mean?' I ask.

'You get to play again. And yet some more. And more. And drink and drink. And lose – be sure you'll lose.'

In the streets – a few tired guys. The bars are locked by day, as if there's something valuable inside. And I am rich, the richest guy in town, and here's the paper, with its puff of gold that tells how much, how very much, I owe. I'm worth.

Night after night. And win and drink and drink and lose.

Elsa says, 'You're quite a character here.'

I say, 'I've nothing else to do, but I'm rich – I'm theirs, and they are mine.'

'The guy, Saleh, who's always with you, guide, tempter, parasite?'

'Yes, that's him.'

'He's done you bad,' she says.

'Yes. Everybody needs him, I've been seeking him forever.'

'He tells you good and bad, and lets you choose the bad,' she says.

'Exactly. He's the one, the irreplaceable.'

'He's unappetising.'

I tell her, 'You're not hungry enough. Only at the end, the very end, can you make the choice, discriminate – the good throw from the bad, the twisted cue from twisted cue, the spheres that aren't quite round, that skitter off ... The bad food from the putrid. What makes you sick from what will kill you quick ...'

Saleh says, 'I can take you to my home.'

'Is this a queen?' I ask.

'No, it's the ace of swords.'

'You guys should get more cards. Have done with mixed heritages, France and Naples,' I say.

He says, 'I can tell you about my uncles.'

'The prison in the desert? Cousins fumbled underneath the stairs? The evenings on the roof, the smell of musk and Cuban cigars?'

'No cigars. But then, my mother ...' he insists.

'A worthy calling. Motherhood. My own, the best in the market. But are these cards the French ones, or the Neapolitan?'

'You're doing bad. We're down. But then – my ambition for doctoring, my impressions of New York ...' he presses on.

'We're up a bit on billiards.'

'It could be a poem. My life, all written down ...' he opens the prospect.

'Yes, no doubt. A noble calling, that.'

'A novel ...' he suggests, 'Carthage deleted. Our children all devoured ...'

'That too. I had bad times with knucklebones,' I say.

'Your wrists – they're too fat.'

'I own these places now. I owe them millions,' I say.

He says, 'It's a worry for you. I can show you family photographs ...'

'I know, the war of liberation stuff. It's all been done, and still – a noble calling, that.'

'Or I could do it as a play,' he says.

I say, 'My guys'll help you throw a theatre up.'

'Your guys, the prospectors ...'

'That's what they are?' I ask.

'You could use them as collateral.'

I'm thrilled, 'You see! A genius! Those magazines about New York – they've borne their fruit!'

'You can sell their souls,' says Saleh. 'Do what you like, they're yours.'

'You're brilliant,' I say. 'Four thousand bodies, even more, with all accessories, the spades, the kids, the sheep, they'll keep us in the game.'

'Why not go home to Elsa?' he says.

'You'll regret you even thought it. Count the pips on this one – there's another stuck beneath – that counts as one or two?'

'My story is a moving one,' Saleh says. 'It could do with print.'

'Forget it! It's the same as all the rest. You're just a gambler's moll. And you're the best. It's time for trictrac now, I feel.'

'You threw it all away. And now, for trictrac you must be relaxed.'

I tell him, 'Then off with all this writing down, and whether boys or girls is best in families – just leave it all to history. That's the decisive one.'

He's disappointed.

Later, I say to Elsa, 'There's no fruit here, but there's snakes. It must be paradise. So, search no more,' and laugh.

She doesn't laugh: 'The search?'

'Is done,' I say. 'It's each one who decides – you win, you lose, you throw it in, you leave the table, dodge the guys that wait outside, you put your winnings in your shoe, your losings – put them in your heart. And off you go – enjoy the musk, those tamarinds, the wise owls that flutter up and down and call and warn and remonstrate. And so to bed – a bowl of figs beside your head, for when you wake ....'

'Then off! – another day of chance and booze,' she says.

'Exactly. That is it,' I say. 'I should have played the three of cups.'

'It doesn't matter. They cheat. They've played together all their lives.'

'I'll beat them.'

'Now you're just initiate. Wait till you're a true worshipper,' Saleh says.

'The throw of the dice, fall of the cards. Design. Mystery,' I say.

'You've got it. I'll be your guide.'

'Elsa doesn't like it,' I say.

'She wants off, on a journey. People change, she

wants to be one of those.'

I say, 'People don't change here. They die.'

'One day someone comes,' says Saleh.

'I'm not convinced, not convinced that's good.'

'We don't hold our breath – it's too precious to hoard,' he says.

'It's all there is,' I say.

'Do you expect more?' he asks.

I say, 'I'm thirsty. More booze.'

Elsa says, quite angrily, 'You'll never pay them your losses.'

'The same with my winnings. They'll never pay. It's the game that counts.'

'They'll all be after us,' she says. 'Them and the four thousand.'

I say, 'I pay the gamblers with prospectors. Live souls. Priceless – ask any humanist.'

She says, 'It's not real intimacy with them – you're just the wall. They bounce their frustration off you.'

'I won't explain the mystery. That way, it wouldn't be. It is my life,' I say.

'You should be off exploring,' she conciliates.

'Those mountains! Carrying all that stuff! Or

paying someone!'

'You don't climb, you walk!' she says.

'At least I don't let boyfriends slip through my fingers.'

'Back again to that! Let's not argue about mountains.'

'It's as good as any subject,' I say. 'The view from up is less an inspiration than the view from down. From up – it's just a plain, all flat. From down ...'

She says, 'It's about striving, not the view.'

'Elsa, we're digging monkeys. That's how we got rich and feisty. Down. Dig,' I say.

'Aha, you're the sage again.!'

'Honing my ignorance to its finest point!'

'You'd best ask father for the cash,' she says.

'No, no, I'll not crouch down, I'm here until I'm paid to leave.'

'The camels are coming! Races!' Saleh says.

Elsa persists, 'The rich ones will want their money. That's how they got rich.'

'Don't be dull about things,' I say, 'Better for you, beached here, than tossed about among the waves.'

*

The desert is a place of contemplation and austerity. It changes all the time, it seems its time has never changed.

Elsa says, 'Time is all around. We are made of it.'

'That's why we must escape.'

'Dig it up, it's patrimony, time forgotten, time remembered, it is all the same,' she says.

The guys here sell the stuff they find. It's time indifferent, without a name.

Saleh says, 'You know, I study.'

'Tell me,' I say.

'Study the truth. Why study anything else. And suffering. For the same purpose – truth.'

'I can't object,' I say.

'The guys here think – you're a wise guy,' and he smiles, his face an egg cracked open. 'A rich Russian. Maybe a Chinese. With lots of answers, hardly any question.'

'That's not the truth, I promise,' and I go on, 'I'll start my accumulator just so ... Camels! What luck: Son of Africa, then Queen of Aksum ...'

'The arrests, closer and closer.'

I think, 'Never go to their houses. Never touch their women. Never pry into their ideas.'

'The prices! The torture,' Saleh says.

I tell Elsa, 'Think of evening in Davos – that's worse than here. And that Ukrainian woman – the torment. Party while you can.'

'It's not good,' she says.

'Remember what we are. Monkeys! With the fear of death. And lots of means of hastening it.'

At times, when there is daylight, I can forget my passion. Chance.

Arm in arm, Elsa and I, we walk along, the sea is over there – things we don't want to see we just ignore and walk around. We could be king and queen, if only for an hour or two. It's long enough.

Camels.

'That tall imperious one, with the knock knees. That's mine,' I tell Saleh.

'A cunning choice.'

'You'll see, Saleh. And then that female in the truck, she's tired and lying down, to gather strength.'

'I've every confidence.'

'The thing with luck is – if it doesn't come and nestle with you, it just isn't luck. Luck's all around. It's like unhealthy sex, you wouldn't want it all the time, it loses taste, but you must seek it. It's our nature,' I tell him.

Elsa says, 'No one walks along the shore like you.'

'That's because I know I had a home, and now I walk and look, and everywhere is home,' I say.

She says, 'The people here feared the bad things – people – coming from the sea. Or the interior. Or the state, when it came, wherever it is.'

'You have to look, to gaze, avoid events. And don't ask any question you can't answer for yourself, to your own great satisfaction.'

'Gaze at the people, stone and bronze, on pedestals? Street names, if there are?' she asks.

'Nice,' I say. 'They don't interrupt you as you walk. Now, go up here, and through this garden – if that is what it is, and mind that dog. See the green in those bricks – that's mud from the river, long ago.'

There's nothing dangerous here, it's all laid out for us, the guys asleep or all at rest, studying, suffering, the truth is all around, but not for us. It doesn't interest. Walk on, walk on. I say, 'Look at the French blue in that tile. All brass, that dusty plumbing stuff. That's a big lizard – there she goes, such anxiety, such little scraps of food they get ...'

'It's a waste, really,' she says.

'If you want me to bury myself to pay for your babies, you can just fuck off. That's not the plan,' I say.

'I wouldn't ask you. Maybe when Nick comes, he'll take a hold ...'

'There's always people coming, good and bad –

there's no selection to it,' I say. 'Those leaves up there
– they look like animals dissembling. Maybe some are.'

Here's Nick. 'Nick, good old friend. You're the lock
for all our doors.'

'You've screwed up here. Your crew, that
vastness – how they must hate us.'

'No, no,' I say, 'They like us all, they love –
they're bound by – their illusions – and, they've got
their spades.'

He says, 'And if it's guns, we'd have a war. What
can they do?'

'Diamonds, or archaeology. Oil, irrigation, gold, a
city.'

'But they live so bad,' he says.

'They have their market. And the study, and the
suffering. What more is there?' I ask.

'You've picked up Elsa. Her tentmate that took
flight ...? I have some doubts.'

'I promise, my libido was a frozen zero. No
motive, so no murder – that's what they say. Elsa –
she's a lovely girl, all flesh, and eyes – those eyes
alone are worth a kingdom and a war! The way her
tongue at times is, it seems, too big – but nothing
animal or in excess, just bursting forth,' and here I

stop, I think of camels, really Elsa is of finer stock, though not so quick or useful, and Nick goes on.

'You've stirred them up, these guys.'

'Nick, it gets so hot here, hot as you'll ever want. No one gets stirred for long. And as for me, I work at making money every night. No coups, ideas or guns – those always get away and run where you don't want it. Faster than a camel,' and I'm back here, at the races, speed and time are one, it seems they should be separate, but when it's camels – the winner makes some history with its time, the rest is casualty.

Elsa is sticky, but she has her dreams, the cherry orchard kind, but nonetheless a dream. Old Nick is heavy, though, as heavy as a tree that falls and blocks your road.

Nick says, 'All you can want in Africa, all that serves, is cash or revolution. Or making them live longer – you don't have the gift for any one of those.' Then he adds, 'First, we must find out how much you owe.'

'That's what I'm worth: my credit, plus my honour.'

He doesn't grasp it, says, 'Owing's what you can't pay. We must dislodge those guys.'

I say, 'No one expects a payment: here, those sums are wonderland.'

'Dislodge.'

'My city. My big hole. My army, my estate,' I

say.

He says, 'You can't go all over making debts. Herding some guys.'

I say, 'You can if you're poor and noble, and your friends are poor. If you're rich, you do it anyway.'

'You're vulnerable. And so ...'

'Are you.'

Nick says, 'If so you think.'

'To me, I'm a success. Big man. And on the brink of crushing victories,' I say.

'Camel victories.'

'You've no idea how valuable and rare those camels are,' I say.

'But they're not yours.'

'I don't think like that. I give them trust. They run as fast as possible.'

'OK, it's true. Wagers aren't real,' he says.

'Everything else is.'

I tell Elsa, 'They found Sabrina in a pot. Cut up. More stewed than roast.'

'That anthropologist? The blonde?' she asks.

'It's quite a cult, the anthropology,' I say. 'They come and sidle in, and want your trust, then mediate with all the other worlds. That pot was silver, like a trophy.' And I suspect, 'Oh no, not the cup for camel derbies,' and I say, 'The pot was fused with all her – stuff: it made an object, you could call it art.'

'It makes a stir – an awful thing,' Nick says.

'It's quite a mafia trick. Quite classical – those urn cremations – you weren't just folded up, they had to decompose – to deconstruct – you, then they stuffed you in,' I tell him.

'You must have been impressed.'

'It was the eyes, you seemed to see them, looking up – so angry, or so peaceful, the question eternal or irrelevant: you clearly couldn't tell,' I say.

'They must have seen her in the bars.'

'I never really heed the passers-through. Best not to pry.'

'It all ends there?' he says.

'The eyes. The eyes will be remembered – though of course, you couldn't see ...'

I tell Saleh, 'There's too much negativity. Nick sees the debts as punishments. Besides, my bank is dead, or else the credit's over. On, on we go, until there is no further, and you can call that end, or destiny. Eternity's all over in a flash, so what you want is immortality – that's the slippery prize that you don't know you've got until the very last, the teetering instant when – with a grin – it slips between your lips, and on to someone else... Those debts are jewels! No use, and no intrinsic value. The value's mine to make, it's what I put on them. The guys who play and win – they're all puffed up, and if they lose, well, it's the passion! Elsa doesn't like the risk – so, what's she living in? You fall, the slope accelerates – and then you find the meadow, blue streams, the geese committees, arms outstretched in welcome ...'

He cuts me off, and says, 'It's time to meet the banker.'

Dr Murad stands behind his desk. The room is hot, we can't believe he spends much time in here.

He says, 'That Sabrina now – she was a scout, though not a good one – looking for a place to build casinos. What disaster it would be, for all you backstreet guys, you gamblers – the rich come in and drive away your sport. Besides, we have a contract with another bunch, much more convenient for us, and so – the moral is, don't meddle, or you'll end up in a pot. Even a silver one.

'Those eyes,' I say, 'or what they'd been, all deconstructed, their blue, fled to the sky! Mark of eternity, but not for her.' And so we pause, and harmonise a sigh.

I say, 'I hope the races will go on?'

'Of course. But in your honour, as you leave. We

wish you well. Those who you owe will sort it out with those who owe to you. Before you go, I have a new delivery,' and he makes a cradle with his arms – no doubt he's family somewhere – and says, 'They send us cash to keep here in our safe. It's safe! Haha! They don't do sums, it's only paper – they don't ask to have it back – although it's beautiful, with views of here and there, and heads of she and who ...'

We go down to the cistern underneath the bank. It's full of pots that look like urns for burial, with labels, noughts and runes and such.

Murad says, 'Look, look here – this note's the highest, right? A million. You fill the currency type in here, when you need the cash. And look – the colour's leached. This was the sun, a rising one, I guess, and here the mountain, maybe belongs to someone else, it's just across from ... over there, anyway, doesn't belong to that lot either, with its venerable cap, so high you've never seen the like – though Europe has them too, I guess. The mountains. The sunrise has leached into it. Red snow!'

I say, 'Well, anyway, I'll take some bundles, just for curiosity.'

The Doctor says: Wait. I'll get some sacks. They'll do for both of us.'

~ II ~

So – I leave, just for a while.

Alone in the desert – a Strato Chief for night-time stretching out. A Robinson umbrella, heavy, made of goatskins, rooted in the sand – under it I pass the days.

Robinson – screaming out the psalms – to be still more alone, but listening for a monstrous voice somewhere – that never answers. Maybe in silence enjoys the racket. In appreciation – sends a black slave.

Screaming someone else's words – that's not for me.

I create a quiet interlocutor, internal. More intelligent than me, to put the big questions, jokes ...

We all go to our deserts, our Siberias, in search of guilt for crimes we've dreamt and not committed. Exiles – but intent on coming back. Some Siberias are colder than this desert's night, but in summer, there's mosquitoes, big as garden spiders – and such heat ...

I say, I think, we say – my self speaks to my other self: 'Between me and me, what are we here for? In this desert. Not to seek wisdom, that's for sure.'

'Wisdom shouldn't need a special place.'

'Elsa says, "For your own safety" – but this here's

not safe.'

'You could seek and not find – and then instruct.'

'Instruct! – it's prowling round a parking lot, trying every car to find one that's open – when there is, you start the motor, but it won't drive off!'

'There's money. That's a key.'

'Ephemeral. And if you don't spend, it's coin. Those notes I took – you write whatever value you prefer, but then you find no one else agrees, and they're worth dust.'

'You could collect coins and turn them into money.'

'That's a cheap trick.'

'Or, if you're tired of buying tat, you could finance a woman, and she'll do the buying for you.'

'That's relationships. Relationships aren't based on feelings – you have feelings by yourself, they are yours, within. They don't impinge outside. Structures are the things that count – the travels, orders, budgets, houses, sometimes a call to arms. That's what binds. Not what you feel, or don't.'

'Feelings do come in.'

'They're round you all the time, and in you sometimes – but so what?'

'You block that path.'

'There's giving orders. That's quite fun.'

'But only if you are obeyed – and who obeys? The idiots, intelligent idiots. And if you're not obeyed,

you end up on a lance. Too risky, that, or else you're
only king of cretins.'

'Or a queen ... There's civilisation.'

'Empire. That means – fine filigree work, some
plays, and tons of slaves and bodies, processions of the
terrified.'

'It seems to me – it's all ephemeral. That, and
ennui.'

'I think you've found the truth! Eternal, fixed –
you find it if you're in a cave or up a pole, a drunk in
doorways or a living god. The permanent's ephemeral.
There! I've done the puzzle – time to go home.'

'The battery's flat. The food they left is crap.'

'That too ...'

'Perhaps it's that worn-out carb, that pinhole ...'

'No, it's the battery. Walking time for us.'

Here's Elsa. I say, 'I walked by night. It looked like I
was asleep, but if I'd really slept that means the
dialectic stops. No contradictions. Impenetrable for
sure. It's true by night I gamble, but the lights are on,
eyes open. I walked and thought by night – you close
your eyes, or else you walk in circles. Close them, you
never know distractions – and here I am. As full of
being as a plum. An egg. No one looked at me, no one

to look at. There could have been people, animals, all round, passive wise men, or warriors – you, they, can't hurt someone whose eyes are closed.'

Elsa says, 'Well, you had some safe time. All gone on inside, and no harm done.'

'The Strato Chief is done for.'

'Only the battery. It sleeps six. Suspension like a rocking horse.'

'It was my sled, faster than the wolves we don't have here. Off into exile – they say "internal exile", as if there is some country, some outside, that's home. The Strato Chief was home, the only home, but it's not safe, not welcoming. Siberia, the desert – it's a prison that enfolds you with its vastness – the snow, the grass, the tiny trees as thin as calf legs, you can't make fields from all that space. It stretches, it's home to nothing, things move through, and so you can't escape. It has no bounds, no walls, no guards. It's all like everywhere. You run and run, you're never out, beyond. No God, no punishment. Just being there forever, expanse inescapable, too big, no differences, without a comma and without a plot. Desert, steppe. No cruelty even,'

I lighten up, 'That's wonderful, isn't it? Just hot and cold, and sleep enclosing, then to wake – under my faithful Robinson shelter, my parasol ...'

'It's not particularly faithful,' says Elsa.

'If you grip it hard, it doesn't have the choice.'

'Lie down again. Try some more sleep. Then you can play some hands.'

Much sex, but not with you, Elsa. Much violence – but clowning and shouting. Much screaming at the sky, and at whoever's up there, hiding. Sleep, Robinson, dream of the brand new.

It's all new, it's all yours to change, this island where you find yourself. You change it all, jiggle the implements, the priestly ones, and wave the sword – now, quick, put the snake in this fine box, place it on the altar. Now you've done all that you could do, all you can be expected to. Just wait, and if it comes out wrong – pretend again: it's new, it's young as you, and so – jiggle the sword, and write, dictate, the rules for living in this place – it looks like desert, but it could be tundra, there's not a monument, a fence to set a limit, it just goes rushing on, down to the sea and then you float – here's deserts, forests, something new you've seen before, and so – more instructions, how to live here, time to bring in punishments. Retribution should be orderly, regular, and not inscrutable. Then, just by living here, there's suffering enough...and those are camels, could be reindeer, some snakes, some wolves, just let them do what they were doing, close your eyes, and if you're not asleep it looks as if you are.

I've got four thousand guys out there, just waiting for a scheme, a purpose, then they'll be off, all racing for the trophy – winners being led, high-stepping, down the red clay road where stay-at-homes are throwing roses, a roaring like the sea. At last.

Elsa says, 'You're no good at contemplation.'

'That's true. But no help.'

I think of the scores of Strato Chiefs out there, the flat muzzles pointing out to nowhere, each cadaver a rusty metalled bronze. Meditating on their past. There is no glory there.

'Where's the guys?' I ask.

'At home. The bars were closed, the truth was sighted, that's why we sent you off. Now everyone is home, to study and to suffer.'

'I escaped all that.'

'They say each got a computer. Now they look for God,' she says.

I say, 'I thought you started off from God, then reasoned out the rest.'

'They say they play. Poker online. But that's no fun for you.'

'There's no power here. Except to close the bars,'

I say.

I think of trudging to Siberia – first the punishment, then the crime. Crime of doubt, *lèse majesté*.

I say, 'Meditation makes nothing happen.'

She says, 'Things will happen. But – your contemplation! Just a pocketful of sand!'

'I'm a spiritual consultant now,' says Saleh.

'Well done,' I say, 'That's the spirit.'

'The cards, the racing, the beer, all gone. We're building the iron man.'

'Your phrase,' I say.

'New order. Or – the old order everyone's forgotten. You need to read it up, the past, and no one does. It's all different, anyway, the here and now.'

'It sounds desperate,' I say.

'This eternal return – it puts a brace on history. Or – it uses history to put some order in the future.'

'History is slippery.'

'It's not the sort of history you mean. The sort you have,' he says.

'I understand,' I say. 'It's a story. Like cards. The system. We, we the others – never found it.'

'It's without memory,' says Saleh. 'This story. So

it's cheating.'

'The armed men?' I ask.

'They're always around. Stupidity. A fad. Passing. Always returning.'

'And not to do with me,' I say. 'I don't belong. And I don't want to.'

Saleh says, 'It's absolutely not for you. Exclude yourself, and we won't have to.'

'My legion, my guys?'

'We'll find something else for them, more wholesome.'

'You're a big cheese, Saleh. I'm pleased for you. And the other cheeses too.'

'We're inventing a good past,' he says. 'The good life, for the right people. A good place to start off from.'

'I envy you. If I go back, to where I'm from, it's just down and dark. Goldsmiths and slaves.'

He says, 'You should choose better, more discriminating. Life's not for tourists. I don't ask "What is to be done?" – I do it.'

'That's not new.'

'Nor is "the permanence of the ephemeral". Elsa tells me everything. Those old automobiles, for scrap!'

*

Maybe I should be a magus, put on the right hat, think again of easing out my long bones, causing wonder, mister miracle – a following for sure. No father writing to my bank, no mother – though she's best that he could buy, she's now – her memory discarded – indifferent, lying somewhere in a bed.

I warn Saleh, his project quite precarious – 'Too many salesmen thrusting round, Saleh. Too many persons, personalities, every one is wanting one, all actors waiting for their line. All different.'

'That is all ending, it must end. Yes, there's too many subjects, persons. You can't listen to them all. Let them be humble, live good lives and do the right. It's the hive, not the buzzing of each bee. And if you're called to dig – you don't declaim instead. No one expects it. And when you play, like we did, when you game – it should be all a rite: – no chat, no chatter. Just enough – the gesture, repeated with your heart gone dead but open to the wind that blows away ... It's gambling to win that isn't right, and it's not humble, winning, losing. Not in line.'

'It all falls down, Saleh. Your project. Living the good life. It's beautiful and doomed, you've picked a species that's quite wrong. We're cannibals, Saleh, and chefs.'

'I'll make a stand, we'll all resist. And there's an end. The end.'

'It suits you, Saleh, I see that. Skulking doesn't.'

*

I say to Elsa, 'No money. Not much hope. I'd planned to make a movie, with my guys, while we were on the way to something else. The "Empire of the Amazons" – true, the queens were ladies, but they'd recruited guys as well. The lost ones, so many ginseng roots, cleaving each other as they run about – the queen commands. A chance for nudity there! Tents with carpets, love with clothes, the feasts, the jousting. It's an epic, Elsa! It's our story!'

'Hmmmm,' she says.

'It's art, if it's done artfully,' I say. 'Rich stuff – our public is in Europe, people read *Anna Karenina* as they commute to work, *Dead Souls* as they are coming home. Elsa – the rules are there in place, they hold: the people bow their necks, listen to tsars and commissars – that's faith enough. The judgements and the hells are all laid out. They've armies and they've bombs enough – Europe is full of them, they don't need more: – a continent that's like a tortoise with its head quite tucked inside. It's all as tight as it can get ...'

'So,' she says, 'Your crap idea won't change a thing? I shouldn't bother then.'

'I'll call you Rodion,' says Elsa, 'because someone in *Crime and Punishment*'s called that.'

'You know that's not my name – I've got a good one tied to me already,' I say.

'Aren't you the luckiest man! You don't have to pay your debts, nor your army. You're in a place that's not New York or Tucson, you can't believe in God or anything the people here have to. They're looking for rules and order – you have none. Now, you can't gamble, so you can't be clubbed to death. You've a mass of cash that you can't spend, that can't devalue. Do you want to film some story – of mutilated queens who squabble over nothing, some bush, red sand?'

'I guess not. We've no cash, though. Just notes in sacks. You're right! This is paradise. But I'm hungry.'

'That will pass,' says Elsa. 'The great thing is, that here you're safe, until they come for you. And that will take an act of will, not a mistake, or chance.'

I start to admire her. She's something special. If only she'd not pitched the tent on overhang, on nothing. Or maybe pitching to her own advantage. I say,

'If you want to get rid of people, how'd you propose ...'

She doesn't respond. I think of Sabrina's eyes, where they had been, potted: looking up into the nothing.

Elsa says, 'We have to eke things out. As a Russian, you know the punishment always precedes the crime.'

'In the books, the punishment is the crime.'

'That's just because they're books,' she says

briskly: 'The real punishment is the uncertainty. Here, something bad will happen, but not yet. I saved you, didn't I? Sent to the desert, all for your own good.'

I think, 'Crap food, no water,' but I do not speak, don't break the spell. What a fine mane she has, foaming – they call it *moutonnant* – down to her shoulders, like the entowered princess, like the flock at sunset, shot by the sun. What an enchantress, what a saviour! I'll keep quiet about the Amazon queens, and she says, 'You need to know when to be up and gone, not thinking all the time about your destinations.'

'Sometimes the big cheeses give you one,' I say.

'Come, Rodion! You know how to jump off a train, better than the others!'

'Sometimes it's a plane.'

'You give yourself airs,' she says. And she laughs. Good teeth, she has.

I'm for luck, she's for calculation – serious stuff, she strives for Capital.

'We need some substance, Elsa,' I say.

'Don't get me wrong, Rodion. I'm big time.'

'In what? You aren't. Besides, I thought I was.'

'Not if you're Russian,' she says.

'Maybe I am, and maybe not. I don't know what it means.'

'Exactly,' she says. 'You don't know what big time means.'

'You just catch me out. What are you in? Traffic,

programmes? Not music or dresses – not seriously?'

She eyes me. Yes, she could do Queen. 'Certainty,' she says.

'You'd need a lot of books for that,' I say.

'Evaluate. You look at what guys think, what they think they're sure of – then you see how it will crumble, split: the rarity of it, foundations if it has them. You don't invent a thing, they do it all. Evaluate what they think is permanent – how long, how well, the rites, beliefs, can last. It crumbles, all splits up, you see.'

'So you say,' I say.

'We've seen the drop, looked over – down it goes, there is no ground down there to stop you. We've seen it all, end of the world, spits in the eyes of all the deities. We know one day we'll all go over, all our arms and legs a-twiddle, termites without their heap. What matters is – how fast the drop, how long there is ...'

'To go,' I finish for her. 'It's all about red snow. You know there's something bad, when that comes down!'

'Exactly! It's not complicated. You need a bit of height, detachment. Mixture of genres – to figure it all out. And breathing steady.'

She's a risk manager, so it seems.

'I think we should dump Nick,' I say. 'He's good at managing resources. We have none.'

'We need a ship. I can't ride camels – the motion makes me vomit,' she says.

I say, 'You're supposed to be the tough one – now you come out with camp.'

'I sold one of your notes. They're what are called collectable. As money, they are duds. As paper – there's a market.'

'Yes! If it's time to go, let's go at once. We'll use the bags of notes to float us out. "Red Snow Imperfects" – they will save us,' and so ...

We leave the shuttered bars, marked cards, the terra cotta walls, the guys all quivering with the word and doing good for once and putting history to rights.

I tell Elsa, 'I'm not at home in water. Never had a mother, nor a birth, and so this swimming thing is alien.'

She's out ahead, those sacks of cash are floating high, and I lose hold. I sink. I'm sliding down. The scene's all marble, white and blue, thick chunks of stone, the size of fists, it turns to pink and purple brawn – I pummel it, inside I turn to fire, I take a drink. I'm not right down, but up is closing, calming down and everywhere is tall bronze doors, the bells sound graver now. There is no ground – what would I use it for? and then – here's Elsa, and she says, 'I got you by the hair. You say you know about a coup, a putsch, but when it comes to drowning, you don't know a thing ...'

'That swimming – looks so simple, just wave yourself about and think of fish. It seems it doesn't always work.'

We climb aboard the ship. We set the sail, whatever makes it move. To Europe!

'You see,' says Elsa. 'The water's not so easy.'

The Captain says, 'One of these notes will do me fine. We're all collectors here,' the sailors press around, the Captain pushes off their fingers and their thumbs – 'It's of the highest rarity, and mint condition,' and we don't say we've thousands of them.

Elsa tells the Captain, 'I manage risk,' and then she looks at me as though to say, 'but not his sort – his is just luck' – and I am humble, trusting, as she means she calculates what Capital might hope to win and lose, and I feel the need to play, desire is in my fingers as if the cards were whisky and the chips were gin and round the trictrac we passed not pieces – as I call them, 'men' – but vodka. In my heart I drink and play, and we are rats on poison, now, our bellies swell, the destination's lost, the project too.

And the desire is on me, and I need the company; dead souls in bundles, and the carriages, over the stone roads, serfs with their little orchestras, a girl will sing a song and follow you for life ... and I would free them all, one hand, one hand would do it all!

But Elsa says, 'You nearly got away, there in the sea. Now we'll go back, back to the bible lands of

Europe, as they stood four hundred years ago or more. Thirsty for rules and faith, they are. Thirsty for it,' and I think how swimming should be easy – in the movies now the guys can fly, and that is surely tougher than the sea.

Elsa says, 'The Captain wants more notes.'

'One's worth more, much more, than ten.'

'We ought to burn the lot. That way the risk is zero,' she says.

'We'd burn our luck. Besides, our risk is always just the same,' I say.

I think, when Elsa calculates the risks, it doesn't mean a thing – we'll play and play, and risk will come and go, but we'll sit on and on, one day the serfs will all be free, and risk will come and go, and they will dig and weld and drive, and we'll play on and on ... But this I do not say aloud, as Elsa's working on the sects, the popes, communions and funerals – and we must find a way to land, to leave this ship behind, its sailors who won't play a hand, or knucklebones, or any sporting thing. That ship! – the swimming that it seems to do, pulsating, motion makes me feel quite sick – and better far the camel with its winning ways, cool style, white as a bone, precarious design.

'When I grabbed you by the hair and saved you – did life flash through your mind?' she asks.

'Many lives – not mine,' I say. 'There's Lenin, getting off the train ...'

'And were his pants too long, just like he said?' asks Elsa.

'We were all shorties then. The revolution was supposed to make us grow, and then our pants would fit. Then there were Decembrists – boots and tall hats. You couldn't tell about their pants.'

'Regression, but no second life,' she says.

It's useful in her work, to know about the resurrections, family happiness, the like.

She says, 'Nick's resenting being dumped, and now he's plotting. Poor Saleh is under threat, but he's got cover – now Nick's after us, it's his crusade.'

I say, 'He won't find us, since we don't know where we are,' but Elsa says that doesn't matter, it's the hunting down – you don't know where the wolf, the whale, is hiding, but you get one in the end, it just takes patience and a single mind, blood on the snow or in the foam.

~ III ~

'Well,' says Elsa, 'Here we are in Germany – the Captain made a detour when I gave another note. The people here – they shout and crow, like Penthesilea dying.'

I say, 'It's clear, that when it all falls down, this here will be the last to splinter.'

'We've seen it wobble,' she says. 'The world. And wobbling it will go, on and on, and – greed may bring it down, but greed will shore it up. These guys here – won't let it fall, and if it does, we shall go East. It seems it is our destiny, to watch it hang and dangle, scramble back.'

I say, 'When we went up the snow, up the – your – Venusberg, to watch the end, we also thought we'd find the seeds, a shrub at least, a fruit, of that eternal garden where you don't know, don't care, if you're alive or dead, or being born again. Instead – the snow...'

Elsa cuts in, irritated. 'I got so I couldn't stand that guy. His brushcut hair, his snooty looks, a French cop with a tendency to beat you up – he quite obscured our quest. Besides, a tent's for two, and you were always there, and snoring.'

I'm annoyed, and say, 'At least I bring a touch of

melancholy, not "upward!" all the time.'

'There's nothing here for us,' says Elsa.

I agree, and say, 'Expulsions from the gardens, penitence, the wrath of God, the apple snatched away or poisoned, the knowledge that you're bad – they've gone through it all, here we shan't find an allegory, still less happiness. Only their music stands to show that aliens have visited and left their voices – though what they say's not to be known,'

'That's whimsy,' Elsa says. 'We're in trouble here.'

'They seem friendly,' I say, uncertainly.

'That's because they think you're mafia. Don't speak Arabic – they'll think you're Chechen.'

'I only know ten words,' I say.

'And don't say we're paradise hunters. They're not interested.'

'I miss Saleh, the guys, the fortress – all that, before they got obsessive with the truth.'

'It was like Eden,' Elsa says, 'waiting for the snake. But don't say that, not anywhere. They're not concerned with Eden here – not any more, and so we shouldn't be.'

I say, 'We should have gone elsewhere, a bigger place.'

'No!' she says. 'Big places are just made of crumbly little ones. You spend your life in cars.'

My Strato Chief, its battery, its strength, drained

out ... I scratch my head – my hair is thick and long, just right for grabbing. That's my strength.

'We've trouble with our documents,' she says. 'They're what you need to move along.'

I say, 'It's Nick. We dumped him and he's sour. He's making trouble too for Saleh, his past of booze and cards ...'

Elsa says, 'Oh no, you didn't invent ... The passport! You elevated your paternity!'

'Identity was all in fashion, so I became big cheese, tall poppy. The president became my father. Gaia, otherwise unknown, my mother. You have to have an origin, or else they won't allow you in or out.'

'That's how you got the notes!' she says. 'They thought you were ...'

'Their vanity and fear,' I say.

'So now Nick tells them we're not who ...'

I'm angry, and I say, 'Of course we're who we are. As for our parents – that was over in a flash – we've nothing to be sorry for.'

'But now it's Nick, he knows! he knows! – we're not who we say, but doesn't know quite who we are and so – he casts us in a limbo, where there's cops and guns all round.'

'I need an identity to get out,' I say.

The cop-type guy says, 'If that's a Soviet passport, I'll buy it. It's collectable,' and I think 'Like cash', but do not say.

Instead, I tell him, 'I need to change my father. Possibly my mother too.'

I see the cross, heavy around his neck. He says, 'We all have one father. Just the one.'

Elsa says, 'That makes issuing documents easy.'

'You must know who you are,' he says. 'Not everyone knows who their parents are, and so it's up to you.'

'OK,' I say. Son of God, mother unknown. Nationality – I'd put "divine".'

I think of Son of Africa, camel at pasture somewhere, and at peace.

The cop says, 'You're not divine, just semi-everlasting – and you have landed on the earth, and that's your root. You don't speak any language very well, creatively, and so – what shall I put?'

I think a while. Nationality. 'Put "desert",' I say.

We reach the frontier. Here's another cop, he takes my passport, and there's laughter. The first cop's given money for my other document, I hand the cash over to this cop – and we're out! Out but not yet in.

'They'll have to invent some other categories,' says Elsa, but the joke is getting tired. She grabs me by the hair and stuffs me in her suitcase. Now – we're in!

'Well, here we are,' says Elsa.

The sign says, 'This is a small country. We live

by crime. Please respect us and leave everything as you find it.'

'This could be a resting place,' she says.

I say, 'We didn't make much of Germany. They once had lots of ruins, but they'd swept them all away. The new buildings are all memorials, so – you can't see anything, nor yet forget.'

I lose more of our notes in the casino. Every spin of the wheel they lose value. I say, 'I haven't got the hang of it. Red, black, what does it mean? Stendhal? What does it signify?'

It looks all right here. A palm tree, frangipane. Cliffs with broken cannons, dragged up from the sea.

Elsa hears from Saleh, says, 'Saleh was more fun when he was bad.'

I say, 'He waited for epiphany, and when it came, his old friends remembered how he'd been before. He had to learn new lines, he couldn't change his voice.'

'They all party here,' she says.

'They'll all do other things as well. So let's not pry. Those trucks, those ships by night ... And you?'

'It's all adventure to me here – swimming, climbing, rescuing. I'm free, I don't need to love anyone, nor say I do – then there's the cash I get –

there'll always be a premium for risk.'

'What cash? You get cash, and yet we scrabble?' I say.

She doesn't want to tell. I respect this. After some days of questioning, she yields:

'It's not your business. I don't need share anything with you.'

I guess she's right. I say, 'You're wrong. The feelings ...'

'Come and go. I don't write cheques against them. Remember the anthem, "no God, no Tsar, and no heroes" – you're in there too. No cash for you.'

'That's my anthem, not yours.'

Those equations, vectors – all into her account. And is this love I don't know what it is, or what it's made of? And is it worth a jackpot?

'It's not as if you loved me,' Elsa says.

'No, but cash is cash,' I say.

Saleh's here – 'on mission'.

'Only spies and losers here,' says Elsa.

He stares at my thin envelope, only a pair of 'Red Snows' left. He doesn't comment.

'I give myself to higher pairs of hands,' he says.

I've just come from the tables. 'Raising your

game? That's good. My guys?'

'They've raised theirs too.'

I say, 'I'm sure that's good – but raising means...'

'I know,' he says. 'It's destiny. The risk increases...'

'The risk is just the same,' says Elsa: 'So is the luck.'

He says, 'Destiny eliminates the danger, so I'm not afraid. It's risk and chance that's now in higher hands.'

I say, 'Well, if you're sure. It doesn't seem to me the danger's less. Remember Sabrina! And Nick has something on us both – me as a spy, and you, a sinner. You need repentance of your past.'

He's glum. 'You never stop repenting, and it never is enough. You repent the past, the future too – it takes up all your time,' he says.

It's like the feelings, those that come and go – what I may feel, and Elsa too. I do not dwell on that. Don't want to take the place of that dead guy, although I suppose that's all we do.

I turn to Elsa, ask, 'What chance do those guys have, and Saleh too? Austerity, rigour, all that stuff.'

'I'd say a year or two, and then they'll all be working for The Man. Or else at war. Unless they find a place to dig, and keep it for themselves,' she says.

I think, 'Those Strato Chiefs – they shed a lot of oil, if you could squeeze it from the sand ...'

'It's destiny and politics,' he says, 'I'm here to raise some cash,' and I commiserate.

'I'm still searching,' I say, 'searching for that garden,' not too hopefully, respecting his dour choice.

Elsa laughs at me, and says: 'This guy could get expelled from jail. The throwing-out is easy – being thrown in is hard.'

The casino stairs are steep and slippery. Here's the tower. Saleh puffs up after me. He says, 'This is your job? Five times a day, to call the players to the table?'

'It's quite a sweet idea,' I say. 'We call it "cultural drift", the trace of rite, or prayer, it makes us all, everyone from everywhere, feel at home, alert. Here, at dawn they close, at dawn they open up again. I am the cock who crows to bring you luck, to summon you to play the game, to spin the wheel, challenge the dice.'

'A significant guy,' he says.

'The most,' I say. 'Without me, they just slumber on. The pay is poor, it's nominal – but there's a perk – I get to be the first inside.'

*

The muezzins come to me for tips on how to make the call.

And still they come, they multiply, my crowd, I never thought to see so many, thick as ants – landing from their planes, their yachts, in uniforms, sarongs and suits, and then rush off again, quite satisfied; they've lost, but lived a morning on their hope, with no one doing sums – and I am left alone, with Mister Curly.

Mister Curly always wins, and yet the management adores him, as he sits – white suit, basket of waxy fruit, two parrots in a cage.

'You can forget my title,' he says.

'I didn't know you had one,' – he means 'Mister'.

He is as smooth as zinc, but I am sandpapered down with sun and moon and mountains, beer from Cluj and deserts everywhere.

'You once-young guys,' he says, 'you make me sick. You come here just to lose and then you want to make the movie, metaphors of life and chance – yet you don't know, that here, we have our ... have the ... garden! Here you find anyone who's made a mark. You don't need to be expelled from somewhere else – you do need winning ways, and then you enter into paradise. Or Eden.'

I say, 'You mean, sir, that paradise and Eden are the same? But if you're dead, how can you sin and be get thrown out? And where'd you go? And knowing what you know ...' I think of Elsa's lover, slithering down the slope – calling a phrase of wisdom as he went we couldn't understand.

'Movies!' Mister Curly scoffs. 'All the eternity you can conceive. Immortals on the plastic.

'Here' – he pokes an apple through the bars, a parrot swears. 'Here, if you win, you gain eternal felicity. What the Yanks call "pursuit of gain", and now it's spreading everywhere – but only if you win, here, at these tables will your gain, your win, turn into everlasting life.'

'And that's why here they love you so? You are the only winner?' I ask.

'No!' he says, and peels an Indian fig, it may be made of marzipan. 'There's been a lot of winners. And mostly, guys get in who've been the subject of a recommend.'

'What do they do all day?' I ask, thinking of lengths of whist, eternal happy families.

'They sit around and drink. What else?'

I say, 'Mister Curly, with respect, I'd sooner be a gatekeeper like you, than while away forever in the garden, doing nothing in particular.'

'That's what they all say. Alas, Sabrina – no gardening for her, they say she ended in a pot. And if you wonder, yes, there can be women here – it's just they never win. Your cards – must play them right, and not be caught with nothing in your hand.'

*

From my tower, I look over into the garden. There's a Bath chair, and some young guys, deadheading roses. A painted cat in a basket, a guy who sells icecreams from a cart, he wears a suit the colour of pistacchio. All more normal than normal.

I tell Elsa. She's magnificent, like Athena climbing off the temple. Or Helen, scattering her troubles like sawdust.

She says, 'Paradise? Pistacchio? Mister Curly? You'd believe anything!'

I say, 'Life's too short to question everything. You need rules, rooted in the past, that you can memorise, that flow to your advantage.'

'No women, there, then. Some paradise!'

I say, 'It's like Plato − just needed fall guys for his lectures − women would have done as well. They weren't required for sex, is all.'

'But − they're needed for the politics, you idiot! That's always present. Women lurking there, through history.'

'Elsa, you're beautiful, and beauty's what we love.'

'What we love is beautiful,' says Elsa sternly. 'Try to live up to that.'

'That's much harder,' I say. And more personal.

'I guess you've lost your last Red Snows.'

I say, 'The chill will come again, a sunset squall, and we'll be rich once more. Red Snow Imperfects. That is history too. Besides – you may have seen, the currencies have all collapsed. Only collectable notes are worth something.'

'Yes,' she says, 'I've heard. It's my profession. Too bad the Red Snows have gone. We'll have to live on what we have inside, interior resource.'

I say, 'Saleh should be fine. He has the truth. And the rest too – the tourism, the automobiles. And the guys – living joyful as their fathers might have done.'

'I like your robes,' I say to Saleh.

'It's those goddam pants,' he says. 'They only suit for riding bikes.'

I agree. 'Lenin was fussed about his trousers.'

'Talking of Lenin,' says Saleh, 'your guys and me, we're keen on apostates – prophets various, all that.'

I say, 'Don't do it, Saleh. Stay with your folks, the prophets that you know. Don't get thrown out, though they say that persecution makes you strong. No entryism, and no splitting – that's the rule. You've found the truth – don't be so picayune! Truth comes, like pants, in various lengths, don't hack it all about,' but he insists.

'We want a prophet, not a speculator – a prophet beamed towards the past. The future ones are crap. A prophet who tells us history, and what to do – not how to live; that, we can manage for ourselves.'

I say, 'I'm flattered – as a Soviet Man, the prophecies about the past come freely to my mind. And Mister Curly here' – and I point, he's poking marzipan fruit into the parrots' cage – 'He has a garden that he runs on Soviet lines, it seems. He is the one true socialist, who always wins.'

'No, no,' says Saleh. 'It's you. We want you. It's your destiny.'

'I have a problem here, Saleh,' I say. 'The currencies have fallen down, and now they want a prophet here, right here, that can explain it all, and tell them what to use instead – and what to covet next.'

This is not quite all the truth, but Elsa said, 'I knew the risk, and now I've lost it all – my cash. Yours too, that you weren't to have, but now it's gone, a half was yours,' and I'm annoyed, and say, 'I needed more than half.'

She smiles, and says, 'Your casino doesn't pay a buck, for all its players lose – and yet it must have safes and gold and stuff ...'

I say, 'It's chips and tokens, and the will to lose, as Mister Curly says – there lies the strength. And what comes out is movies, but the cash, the real stuff, that stays in the safe. It can work wonders, Elsa. It's faith that bears it up, a faith like Saleh's, despite all the heresies ...'

'Your passport!' says Saleh. 'It's exceptional.

Exemplary!'

'It doesn't get you far,' I say. 'The father thing.'

'You Russians want to leave when things are good. We from Africa – only when they're bad.'

I say, 'It's the Mediterranean, my home. Back there in Russia – we don't have it – got close with Sochi, but not quite.'

He asks, 'What can you tell the guys, what message? – those guys you promised everything – and then ran off.'

He has a point. I say, 'The games. Your culture things. The games invented – dice and chess, trictrac, cards too I shouldn't wonder – not to mention camel races. And the mathematics, to make it all add up, and fix the odds. There's solidarity, and sitting in the twilight, your mind engaged.'

'Hmmmm,' says Saleh. 'It seems a little limited. There is a down side too.'

'I speak as I see. I saw. I can't do better.'

A little setback.

They bind me like a goat. The Italians have a word for it – my hooves and neck are tied, so if I kick, I strangle.

In the trunk it's dark. Like childhood. When they

take you out, they question you, then there is punishment, the beating.

We bound along, more stony roads, the rocks bounce up, and make a cadence on the underside. Movement's quicker than in hell, the pain is much the same. Will I be taken out and beaten, shot – or left inside, and shot?

Now – here come the questions. Do I believe in floating currencies? – then, deeper still in theory, and I scream – the rope is eating at my neck – I shout, 'No, no, I'm not a boss of currencies, do what you want, and I'll conform.'

I can't hear too well, it's muffled and statistics. I hear ... 'for big sums ... a bride price, for the rest ... it's cigarettes and vodka,' and I shout, 'For a Mercedes then – the price is two women and six cartons', and there's silence. Clicking. Have they got an abacus? And someone here, and small, is breathless too – and soft. And trembling, just like me.

I'm saved! A rabbit, being taken home for dinner. Good old, kind, rabbit. He'll be eaten, I'll be saved, and thank you! They'll never risk a shooting, blind, when the trunk is closed, and dinner is involved.

They've won, the bad guys – no contest – they will hold the bank, decide if payment is to be in tokens or in melons.

Take me home and let me out.

This economics is an easy game, just keep your

nerve. I'm tumbled out. The rabbit and the car, a Buick Skylark I believe, move off – but I am still tied up, it all depends on keeping those knees bent, there must be a curve, equation that describes what currency to use and help you stay alive.

Courage, good people! Help!

I think of Sabrina, doubled in her pot and halved, the bad bits thrown away somewhere, and just the eyes turned up, the sockets, a gesture that we say is hope. The sky.

Someone cuts my rope, and I am free to be a goat again.

'Those rabbits lead you many a dance,' I say, to lighten up the scene.

Someone says, 'It's just some poor lunatic they've taken for a ride,' and that too brings me peace.

My legs have seized. I'm locked in on myself, a safety pin.

A woman says, 'I've seen you in your tower – I know you, so I cut you free. I'm down below, I sell tickets for the garden, by the hour. There, losers pay and sit around in idleness so they won't lose some more.'

I recall the ice-cream cart, the guy, his suit, and maybe her; she's Sonia, and I say, 'It's all a spoof? The garden isn't paradise? Then Mister Curly tells it wrong!'

'People who haven't sinned are always being

expelled – there's gardens everywhere. You get expelled over again – people like you, who're ignorant of history, the economy, it happens all the time, around this lovely sea. The people come and go in bands and armies, round and round, and throw each other out, and are thrown in, and all around. It's destiny. And it's quicker now.'

With Sonia, I can talk. I talk to her – the not-so-lovely Sonia – talk about hydraulics, about the restoration of the waterwheel. She calls me Rodion too: 'That's not in your passport, but it sounds authentic.'

I love her, love myself.

I say, 'If I talked to Elsa, I'd soon be sliding down the slope, so I don't talk, I just exchange.'

'You talk to her all the time,' says Sonia.

'It's just exchange. We never touch.'

'She's very beautiful, too beautiful,' says Sonia.

'Yes, too beautiful for me. You might say – she's not ephemeral. She keeps a cautious eye on my – on everyone's – caprice. I'm not afraid of her.'

'I shouldn't go that far,' says Sonia.

'The people round her tend to die. It's not her fault. The tent – that short-haired guy. Sabrina. No connection. All the same ...'

Sonia – no one would want to harm her.

I chase her, chase her away from me, for her own good. For mine. Don't wait for me! and no redemption!

My selfless shoulder, cold as snow, turns in her face. I laugh.

Elsa had said, 'There'll never be red snow again – those were dramatic days, and full of error, now they're past. It's chance – we lost all our cash, we knew we could, we knew we would.'

I told her, 'I won't create another currency. I don't touch those monsters, those machines, that spit out tokens. In chips, in fiches, there is no style. The money's fallen down like air, and now we see a threat that's everywhere.'

Later, I say, 'The only cash I took, it was a gift. Those notes ...'

Sonia. To save her, with great finesse – I push her, push her away, I save her from the burden of myself, I save myself the burden I don't feel like taking on.

'Well,' says Elsa. 'Religion or economics?'

'Religion's more precise,' I say.

'Cheap shot,' she says. 'And you're not a believer. Things could be difficult.'

'So's three people in a tent,' I say.

'It was an expedition. On those, you don't know

what you'll find, or what you're looking for. Inside the tent, or out.'

'Religion doesn't need qualifications,' I say, 'nor psychology.'

'You may have to live in a cave,' she says. 'Alone. If you insist on going back.'

I think – Big men get bigger doing things that they've screwed up.

I hear a raucous voice, it says, 'Kondratieff, Kondratieff, man of the waves,' and it's a parrot. Mister Curly too – bent over a steaming barrel.

'Enjoy your rabbit stew,' I say.

'I shall, most certainly, I shall,' he says.

Elsa says, 'I don't think Saleh wants help with his religion, least of all from you. It's his way of asking for money. All you promised.'

I say, 'He'll be disappointed, then. Disappointment's his profession.'

Elsa says, 'He's so solemn.'

'Just one of the boys,' I say, 'But not your boys.'

She says, 'Keep clear of him. He's trouble. We – you and I – we can make history here.'

I say, 'It's squalid here.'

'Oh no, you're being – who is it? – again. Russian heroes – Uncle Vanya types. They think the sacrifice is not being sacrificed!'

I say, 'Sometimes you just watch the river. Sometimes – over the cliff you go. That should bring things back to you.'

We think of Sabrina, in her pot – not Russian, not a heroine.

'No, not heroic in that way, the lonely victim,' I say. 'But mobilising: setting thousands on the move.'

She says, 'You can't go back there, you're so anomalous. They'll see through you, they'll chew you up, they'll spit you out.'

'Then I'll go alone, into the desert. Avoid being swallowed.'

She stares at me. Her eyes, her eyes. What riches there.

'I think you shouldn't go,' she says.

'If you go high enough, there's snow – and that's anomalous too. In Italy, there's this volcano – so high, there's snow, and in the cracks there's fire and magma, snow and red. Now, that's anomalous! That's life, that's something on the move you don't know where it ends.'

'You've no idea,' she says, 'How trite you sound.'

There's the shore again. Maybe the waterwheel's been fixed. I can't make it out. No camels.

Saleh sees I've nothing with me, no baggage,

envelopes.

'Why are you back?' he says. 'There's nothing for you here.'

'A little friendship – does no harm,' I say.

'Friendship's another thing. Not at stake in this. So, why?'

'Atonement,' I say, although I think I've done nothing that I need atone. 'It's personal. Perhaps a step towards redemption.'

He says, 'Then it's incomprehensible. It doesn't register.'

The town has its own mystery, like it always had. Maybe I've invented it, the mystery.

'Desert,' I say. 'Or mountains. I'll find something. Danger everywhere.'

'Yes, that's for sure – the world is very wobbly,' he says. 'Colours leaching everywhere,' and we laugh.

I set off. The sun is climbing up his stair. Here is the desert, it has come a little closer since I left.

I don't need anyone to calculate the risks, nor watch me.

THE ROCK

If you don't feel that this is your time yet,
don't keep your appointment

Carlos Castaneda,
Journey to Ixtlan

'I want that six-ton block,' I say. 'Though it does have a rusty streak.'

We must push on, as though there's nothing ever ends.

Here in the pit, there's a small mass of people dislocated, disconsolate. Trouble. The young ones blame the older ones: I hear 'uncertainty'. The very old think they'll be deported, or be shot. The middle ones are angry, but they're ready to be deferential.

We look on, Finn, friend and freedom fighter, and me; doing some philosophy to while away the fates of those disoriented guys.

Finn says, 'There's two types of women – the haughty, and the submissive. Both bringers of much pain.'

I say, 'You can't say that any more – men and women all the same all depilate, say "fuck".'

'And men, a single type,' he goes on, 'talk pompous, act like Loki, full of tricks and stab you where you haven't looked.'

He points. 'Over there, on the quarry's furthest wall, that bridge. It's shaky. To test it, and escape – do they all rush over in a scrum, pray that they'll all cross? Or first send fat old guys, who'll not be missed when it falls down? Or light ones, with better hopes and better luck? And if it falls, what then? Do you leave so many starving prophets on their rock? They can't climb out, the quarry's just a hole, they'll stay for ever.'

I say, 'It's a puzzle. I can't wait here and see them sort it out. They shouldn't get into impasses they can't solve. Trapped in a metaphor. Let's have the quarrymen load my rock – and off!'

I do my art here, in this field. Tania, my lover, passes by and asks, 'You hack the lump until whatever is inside's revealed?'

She looks admiringly – describing the miracle's as good as doing it.

'That's what they say,' I tell her. 'Maybe I just pound an image on to it. You mustn't think it's like a pig – when the butcher discovers it's really sausages. This lump is just inert. It doesn't have a "now", not like a pig.'

'So, you think you give it life?' she says. That's not like her, she should give up this mysticism.

'Sausages,' I say. 'Maybe there's just sausages.'

I start the saw. 'This thing must have a clutch,' I shout, it's waving like a wand. A touch, one whole side falls away. 'I've never done this with this thing,' I say. The holes I'd drilled are much too small. I shout again,

'A photograph!' Like a knight, I stand astride my

block, the saw's my sword, its diamond bits a-glister in the sun – and I am off to gouge its marble soul, or stamp my own upon it. Memorial for all the dead, or for some buyer, eager and alive.

Finn snaps me, and I say, 'Send the image round the world, be sure to add my name plus "sculptor", give a title too.'

'That slab that just fell off,' says Finn, 'Would make a summer table.'

I say, 'I'll call the big piece "Mutilation". Maybe gender it, "*la mutilata*" – more edge and resonance. If there's a commission – "The Mutilated". That should cover every bit of history.'

Finn says, 'Frontiers, diasporas. Irridentism and ugly weapons.'

'Exactly,' I say.

He says, 'Maybe the block's a mask, hints at a mystery inside.'

I say, 'That's lazy, sloppiness. Behind the mask there's just another mask.'

'Most people like a figure, human, stripped off if possible.'

'The rock's already naked,' I say. 'There it lay, sleeping within the others. I bought it, ripped it out – it hadn't been expecting that.'

He persists, 'Most people like to think there is a mystery – a flower, an animal, even a skeleton that's trapped inside.'

I say, 'They're wrong. There isn't. Mysteries – they're better left as such.'

The Greeks, the chips of marble that they've left us ... They managed; abundance of tied help, the gods would lend a hand – some chiselling, a striking-down of rivals. Now, with God-in-a-book, we have no need for pictures. 'Don't go back to God,' says Finn.

'Touch of the numinous, nothing more,' I say.

Finn's a dry old kipper. Things are all the same to him. Interests, misfortunes – to him, it's all parades, a procession passing by from there to here to there again – just worthy of a comment. Dry kipper comment, Time's lost, and then remembered. After, it's all parade. He's had his glory, mine is yet to come. He says, 'Don't sniff. My life is history,' then, 'That block's too small for you,' he says. 'You need a bigger lump. But you are fixed on misty things, and whisps, the rituals in black caves. That sort.'

'You're right. This sculpting – we seem to lose the knack. It's all memorials, and shapes left in some garden.'

'I think,' says Finn, 'You should attack it with your hunger – then, treasure it as a possession.'

'Like a piece of cheese?' I say. 'I could put a rat

on it. A brute monstrous bronze rat.'

'Or a silver one. A gold one,' he says.

'A tiny one. Each time, the meaning changes.'

'Cats like cheese too,' says Finn. 'And lots of it. You could put one on, in competition with the rat. Or a rare tiger.'

I shout at him, 'Why you? My public – why must it be you? Everything you say turns it to camp!'

Offhanded, he says, 'Well, being a critic is quite camp. Being a sculptor now – you think it's macho, buzzing over your cube, like it was a mountain, while life sails on – it's quite pathetic.'

'It's what it is,' I say. 'What happened to that sad platoon, down in the quarry?'

He says, 'It seems they sent some oldsters over, testing it, and then the bunch. It all fell down when the last ones, very old, receptacles of memory – went over slow. Too bad for them.'

I say, 'That was the best, the worst, conclusion. Who's to say?' – and really, I don't care, and nor does Finn, my block got out in time, and here it stands, it's up to me to give it destiny.

'I'll leave you with the puzzle,' he says. 'It's a cube, so try rotating it ...' and he's gone.

*

'I saw your images. They're creamy,' says Perry.

'Perry has a gallery, you know,' says Finn. 'Who's not in money here's in art. She's one skinny leg in both.'

The block is full of starts and memories, where I've been attacking it. I say, 'It's brought my parents back – how they lost God and socialism, both. They'd gone for bust, and busted were,' and she peers at the marble:

'Can't see ideology here,' she says.

'Carry it away. Show it to your fans,' I say.

'Hmmm. It's too heavy. The floor ...'

'OK, here's the answer. Land it on the roof – through it goes, and there you have it on your floor. If it persists and goes on going down, you've got an elevator shaft.'

She touches a corner, as if to lighten it. I say,

'The story's in the weight. Like all of us.'

Her resistance grows.

I say, 'I'll get some guys to do graffiti on the lump – almost mixed media so. I didn't make the stone, you know. Mine's just a twist, it stops at surfaces. The guys like you that ponder over it – they didn't make the stone, nor give the twist. They're even further from the root, the source.'

'I'm not interested in the source, the authenticity,' she says. 'If I was, I'd throw some stones and soil around. You'll have to find some other spell – till then, I'm the enchantress. You wheedle me – you haven't got a chance, my space is closed for you,' she says, and stands there, tough and dumb.

'She's an interesting woman, that,' says Finn, condescendingly. 'She's called after Perilla, Ovid's daughter – you know, author guy of "shapeshifting".'

I say, 'That's a musty thought. If she doesn't want six tons, I'll make it sixty, or a line of basalt columns, six hundred tons, big heavy post-imperial ones.'

Finn says, 'She had a circle, got passed round. Rather a tarty thing, she realised – and underpaid. Went to Africa, much sought after, some regal screwing – a rite, I'm told. Then trading guns or running them, then just running, and sleeping rough. Those mattresses! the smell of fish, the jumping things!'

'A tough one? Or is she just a rolled and shiny stone?' I ask.

'It's what we all go through,' says Finn, gloomily. 'But not everyone ends up in art.'

As he goes on, I feel a tiredness with the world – its pebbles, tiny in its image, endlessly reproduced and different every one. No resolution. No bloody swords cleaned in the sand, here the beach, the towers, conquest and pillage. Off again ...

I say, 'I'm giving up this sculpting. If it isn't wanted, let it make its way,' and, inspired, I say, 'Like Perry! Round the world. Without a friend.'

We load the rock on to a ship. No destination. Let it land where it may.

Finn says, 'It could be tombstones.'

'It is a tombstone,' I say. 'Let it sail on, and find a body it can rest on. Someone mutilated, to make the point. Around the world it goes ...'

'Or ends up in the sea,' says Finn.

'No, no,' I say. 'That's not the way. It's cargo, it must potentially arrive and have a customer. It will pass from land to land, in every port will be admired or just passed on.'

'It could be a roadblock,' says Finn hopefully, 'and be shot up. A counterweight – and balance cranes. You see – it's metamorphoses! And even end like Perry, in a gallery.'

'Or a shooting gallery, and be its prize,' I say, dismissing the adventure. And its travesty.

Perry said, 'It's a wonderful job! Believe me! The marble grubbied up, like granite – the rust and oil together, coming from nature, or the saw. Then – those little half faces, scribbled on, and aren't those lions of Nineveh? – so tall, the man attacked and weaponless, is falling back ... it's all memorial.'

Finn says, 'The block is off to sea,' and Perry says,

'There's so many memorials – better that they all go off around the world.'

'He's just another guy – huge vision, strangulated

voice,' says Finn. He points at me.

I say, 'I hope the goddam thing doesn't come back. It's just some ideas, set in stone. The more ideas you have, the less they're listened to.'

'Yours aren't exactly ideas,' says Finn. 'Now, mine was one idea, and it caught on. Build a nation. Here come the occupiers, bringing order, making hell. And then we have our civil war, a liberation struggle, that brings all kinds of hell – then we win, there's peace, there's order – off we go!'

'And you were right,' I say hopefully, 'you're sure you were.'

'On that we can agree,' he says. 'If you live somewhere, that land is yours – ours – not someone else's, along with all the other stuff – the soil, the birds, the parchments and the warriors. All ours. Not equally, of course.'

'Oh, I still agree,' I say, thinking of where my next ideas can sail. Put them in another box, and off to somewhere in the stars, maybe.

'Anyway,' says Finn, 'my liberation struggle – wasn't my country, not my clan, my party – not even my idea for where it was – those boundaries in the sand!'

'It was the big idea,' I say. 'It had to be expressed, and then – on to the next. Maybe another time it's quite the new, the opposite.'

'That's how it goes, yes, the design is that,' he

says, 'you can be sure.'

It's good to find a person to agree with, and I ask, 'If Perry likes my block, then why ...?'

He's angry, and he says, 'Liking? You want it to be liked? A fucking block of stone with carvings on it? Cash and admiration – makes me vomit,' and he does, we hold each other and the street goes round and round, and it's quite a famous scene, even the cops are hovering near, but he has shot his lunch and dinner, and there's nothing more to say or do.

'Carvings!' he shouts, 'After what that girl has suffered, the wars, the mattresses infested ... And still will be, on and on it goes,' and he bares his eyes, red and wet, and points them into mine.

'The masterpiece is easy, it comes natural. It's the fame ...' I say.

'Now,' says Finn, 'why would you be wanting that? Everyone has a bad luck story, everyone is cursed from birth. Those tall towers of tales, they're made to topple over, those tales of monsters slain, prisons endured, massacres survived. The air is full of it – those masters of forgetting, saying "clear the paths, let more tormented masses have their say, and be forgotten" – move on, move on, *davai, davai*! Do what you must, let others count the cost. Fame! A black stone. Others reaching inside themselves to find what they've been told is their humanity! And then, those smaller, grubby stones! Stones to throw at larger stones – it weighs you down, it's natural. The flux – you have to plunge, it rolls and closes over you ...'

'Well,' I say, 'right or wrong, I've had enough of art. And money's too demeaning. The money clan – dim collectors of ebb and flow, tide tables from the world around – the ups and downs of bread and scrape, sometimes a jelly sandwich. Money! It's rise and fall! Watch it – it's surely in that mousehole – see its whisker, tiny eye ...'

'I can't wait to hear you,' says Finn, 'listen to you, say the obvious. Fame. It's fear. Fear you'll disappear, leave not a rag, a smell, a taste, a colour, smudge of dust, a scar, a gene, a forest hut, a bang of something falling down, no mark that's hit ...'

'Right, you're right,' I say. 'It's fear. What's wrong with that?'

'Face extinction like a man,' says Finn. 'After all, it makes no difference.'

We ponder this.

'Talking of black stones,' says Finn, 'if it's money you want, you can have lots, and never put your boots on. Everyone is scared, the tide goes in and out, and no one knows quite why, the fortunes ebb and flow, nature or malice – it is much the same.'

'Tell me,' I say.

'Scared guys insure. They know they're shaky, so they bet their fortunes on someone else's fortunes that may be, well, less shaky. Black bets on red, diamond on spade, cup on sword – and round it goes.'

'There must be some ultimate, some final totem, home stick, stuck somewhere,' I say.

'Of course. It's Mecca, Lourdes, Medjugorje. All the wealth in pilgrimages and palaces – some truth that's triple A, and some a little less. In the last resort, that is.'

'No, Finn! Not religion, not again, even if it's popular,' I say, disappointed.

'You haven't understood. The final bet must be, must seem to be, outside the system. A bank won't make it's final bet on other banks. A paper pyramid will not conceal a corpse. You put the faiths together, in a bundle, the symbols, apparitions, fighting good fights, all that. The best side guarantees the worst side as it multiplies,' he squawks, triumphant.

I say, 'It's all illusion, one on another, piling up. You say you have to play at risk and then you place your faith in hazard! You try to save the world, the trees, by sneezing on your sleeve! No paper handkerchief, no driving Cobras, no eating chickens! It's just a style!'

He says, 'You haven't grasped. The innocent good will bear the weight of all the rest. The cash is handed to you, as the trembling souls seek the last guarantee, the miracle, the certainty. The Word, the apparition. It's the *clou*. What saves the money system is the system that lies just beyond it, makes it all worthwhile and stable.'

He is satisfied, I haven't understood. 'Why? How?' I say.

'The end we seek – it is not there, where we go seeking. The system fails, can't guarantee itself. That "end" is outside the system, where money doesn't count, and is surrendered. To you – if so you wish.'

'But,' I say, 'the virtuous end is really at eternal war. Those battles in the good drive all the rest.'

Finn says, that beyond the illusion – that everyone suspects – there is another illusion, that everyone suspects. But everyone seeks the second mirage, while striving to accumulate in the middle of the first. He believes that to pass from the first to the second, everyone will give us their money.

It seems quite unlikely.

'Have it your way,' says Finn. 'Your defeatist way. A theory must be beautiful before it's true, or else it can never be true. And this one – it's a beauty!'

I say, 'Finn, you've no money.'

He scoffs. 'Some people have savings. I have ideas.'

I say, 'Thinking like that, it leaves you vulnerable, you're on the run, like – there's a guy, they're looking for him now ...'

'Ah,' says Finn, 'how I wish I was that man! I'd make a hollow and lie in it, and feel myself get thin, so thin, and hear their feet around my head, and lie there

with a chuckle deep inside – then, like a salmon, lithe
and silver – through their net I'd slip.'

I say, 'The guns, the dogs. And those awful things
you'd done?'

'A salmon – you don't catch them with dogs! And
purified, with lying in the bracken – just running,
running round, you're sad, a toxic lump, bad breath,
bad mothers, and bad friends. Silver, my old friend.
The wise fish. And lithe.'

We're always on the run, and that is right and
true. Finn says, 'The cops have strictest rules – they
only shoot civilians when they're sure they haven't got
their man.' That too seems right and true.

'It always happens thus,' I say. 'The thing is,
"don't be innocent" or you'll get hit when patience
fails, or politics comes in. Best have your gunfight,
win or lose – or otherwise you're comic, some fat guy
running in the hills and hiding behind trees.'

'You're almost right,' says Finn. 'Although as
usual, formalism's got in – and that's the felony
they'll hang on you.'

Finn repeats, 'If you must go inside, don't be
innocent! Innocence fucks you up, you feel bitter.'

'That must be the case,' I say. 'And you, Finn,
must feel your task is infinite. The liberation
movement – is it still called that? – no sooner done
one country than you start again, from the beginning –
even going backwards. Finishing off some job.'

Finn says, 'Yes, and the same arguments, about the omelettes and the broken eggs, the innocent, expendable, sacrifice of generations – the "getting in the way", "discouraging the others", the honest bigots, mercenary sophisticates,' and I see he's laughing at me, as I laugh at him.

Finn says, 'You know, those soirées,' he pronounces it 'Suarez' – 'that they used to have, just seemed a sing-song? Lady writers, sussing out the values of estates, all that. It seems instead – that as the company trilled and roared, a couple screwed, right there, the pianist pedalling on. And then – another song, another pair, the matrons and the skivvies all, the Austens and the Brontës, indiscriminate.'

'So, "I dreamt that I dwelt in Tara's halls" is just a bordello theme? Where'd you hear?'

It's bursting out of him: 'The Latins, now, they had a hotter repertoire – the *"brindisi"* from *Traviata*, and that song about the railways – "Finnifunny – something". But Sunday evening, nineteenth century, everyone with an instrument and friends – to it and at it, every one.'

'What are you getting towards, Finn?'

'Ah,' he sighs, 'if only I was more attractive, what a time I'd have.'

I say, 'Maybe your self-pity holds you back,' and he is cheered. That's curable, and with some singing lessons too ...

He's in expansive mode, he shows a little box, 'My medal,' he says, so sweet and simple, 'for the liberation struggle. Not that I'm for nations, you must understand. But it's a stage, a necessary stage, and going back is worse. It's like the surgery – you cut and cut, and things will never be the same, but that's the good result.'

'Don't you have a ribbon?' I ask, 'or a hole in it, to put it round your neck? You need a lad who's got a drill ...'

He shows me. Three-quarters back of some draped lady, holding flowers, they could be arrows.

'That seems general purpose, Finn,' I say, although I envy him his history, and there's no way to take that from him.

'Clearly, I didn't do it for this crap medal,' he says.

'Now,' I say, 'here's an odd thing that needs analysis. That's your strong point. There's this lady, who I meet quite casual. Without a word, she takes me to the shop she works in, early morning this – and there, right in the window, which is garnished full – loudspeakers, spying stuff, and telescopes, things that hum in boxes – there we caress and kiss, and then she waves goodbye, and maybe it's a week, a month, there she is again, and – all over me, just like before. Not a word.'

'Maybe she's mute,' says Finn. 'Maybe it's you

the curious one, and she expects a thankyou or some cash. Maybe ...' and he's back in soirées. 'It's her culture, and you're a character in bigger stories – or just a guy that's up for random hugs. No singing?'

'None that I can hear.'

I say, 'We'll never have jobs. We say what we think.'

'Even if we're always wrong,' he adds. 'Or often. But why bring in the truth? We want to choose the context, not the content. Most things are far below us.'

I ask, 'More liberation struggles?

'One is enough,' he says. 'And it's fucking uncomfortable. And you know that higher up there's contradictions and betrayals and travesty. It's all worthwhile and horrible. People have to have their chance, even if they don't want, don't thank. And the big guys get the power, you get dust and aching feet.'

'You sound like a busted general.'

He squints at me, says, 'That's why we're never employed again.'

I say, 'The knights of old – they left their women behind when they went off for quests. We look for ones to take along. There's Tania, now. She minds machines – productive, even.'

Finn sniffs: 'I don't expect she produces anything.

It's the machines that do. She gripes because it's long and boring – I would too.'

I'd shown Tania my marble.

'You say it's rubbish,' she said, 'so I can say it too.'

'No, certainly you can't.'

'You want flattery. That doesn't mean anything,' she says.

'I want respect for past efforts. Projects.'

'I can't,' she says.

'Then fuck you! Finn and his politics – he mocks, maybe, but on the highest level – you do it, and it's just stupidity. You judge the consequences, not the intentions. But it's the intentions pursued that count.'

She says, 'I stand further back than that.'

I say, 'Then you're an angel. And accomplish nothing. And make nonsense of everyone else.'

'Hey,' says Tania, 'besides. Go light on that "lover" bit. If you're not mine, why should I be called your lover?'

'Well,' I say, 'what are we learning, sitting here? The journey calls – once it was guys who knew it all, sitting beneath a cactus, with for sale peyote, or it might be some warm beer. But now airports are full of

monks, forget the countries and the names on stamps –
it's cities now, and universal brands and dictionaries,
bunkies in every railway station – forget the sailor and
their wives in every port – we're off, the crewmen are
all gays, those rockets – up to the stars, the astronauts
too, all gays, or else the pining would be dire. Move
out, Tania, in the stream, let it bear you on, down to
the sea or maybe it's a drain that's making energy, let
go, those hundred flowers will bloom in you – forget
the time when you were one, unique, now you are cut
and polished into tiny bits of glitter. Hundreds of you
flourish where there was only one, one stolid beast,
seeking identity – for what good use, what purpose?
One, integral? What's the sense, there's nothing you
could do about your oneness – better to be splintered
into chips, and mounted delicately on some planchet–'

'Yes,' she interrupts, 'this delicate mounting –
that's what I'm not happy about, want some answers
to.'

I turn again to Finn: 'Come on! You've had your
fling, your victory – against an empire, too. Stop
worrying about your women, think only of your
glory.'

'It would have happened anyway, without me.
And now you want me on the march again – another
dirty fight, maybe with guys who pray! And march
and march. It's all for cash and locks and keys. So be
it. Do it yourself. I shan't cheer.'

I say, 'You've outlived your time, old friend. Perhaps you aren't cut out for relationships, all that, and making compromises, coming home each day – same house, same woman, same sex, same job.'

'Put so,' Finn says, 'who could resist?'

I push forward. 'By good luck, art is eternal, so my interests are quite different.'

'You've just given up the art,' he says. 'Though you could be mister critic – lots of travel joined to that. You like the airport scene?'

'That's true,' I say. 'My destiny's too easy, yours – impossible!'

He's irritated: 'You haven't earned a buck for years.'

I say, 'It's the market. If there weren't losers there wouldn't be a market. A time of transition, that's where we are, a pause in the general eternity. It leaves you hanging there, until.'

'Exactly.'

Friendship, art and politics – we've covered those. And liberation too.

'I've seen it all,' says Finn. 'Eternal recurrence doesn't make it easier. First you fight to save yourselves, and then it widens out. Then, you fight until you've decided what your victory might look like. You win, you lose; and in a year, a hundred years, it's all a different scene. The sadness is the same.'

'You're a master, Finn,' I say, 'but—'

'You don't need hate your enemies, so you don't need love your friends. You – you made sculptures, talking to the rock. With your electric saw. Hoping things pop out.'

'That's about it,' I say. 'But a bleak prospect.'

'Rocks are bleak,' he says. 'They got their reputation so.'

'Finn,' I say, 'I see why you're not liked. You shouldn't say it like it is, you must smooth and label.'

'And satisfy the buyers,' he adds.

'We're screwed, Finn,' I say. 'What shall we do?'

'Forget the woman in the hifi shop. She sounds a chancer. That leaves you with Tania.'

Tania lives in a witches' house. The witches are her parents. The bushes in the little yard bear candied fruit, roses and violets together. The old couple come from out there, somewhere, a March, a Bukovina. They're still out there, that remote somewhere. They sit moulded in their chairs, like Norse chessmen.

Tania introduces me: 'My insurance agent,' and they nod as they register the lie.

'You can't go out,' they tell her. We go out.

'Listen,' says Tania. 'My brother has a problem

with a cop. The guy found lots of hobby stuff, in car and garage, all innocent, for defence, for baseball, things for ethnic games, the bows and arrows. Just say it's yours, I'll go with you wherever.'

'Small house, big brother,' I say. 'I saw no brother.'

'He's a distant brother.'

'It sounds a little thing,' I say.

'Then do it,' she says.

'No.'

'For me,' she asks.

'No. Absolutely.'

'My parents are evil,' Tania says.

'They distrust strangers,' I say.

'They'll only ever see strangers. It's a little house. That's what the working class live in. If strangers aren't allowed, I only have those two, and my machines.'

'Your brother seems to have a problem too. My family lived in small houses, you know.'

'He's been a real brother. Better than a brother, as no blood comes into it. Till after.'

'I guess it's good, for you.'

Nothing is good about Tania, but I think I'll take her, and Finn can have the woman from the hifi shop.

When we've left this place, everyone will seem quite different.

*

I'm in the shop again. Milly. She kisses, holds me without a word. All the technical stuff, it looms above us. I see people looking in the window: I hear, 'Those prices – they're quite mad.'

'You'll like my friend,' I try to tell her. My mouth is stuck to hers. It's not a sexual thing.

'We have to go away,' I say, 'some time away, it will be good, there's Tania, for assurance.'

She's eager, and she says, 'I want to get away myself – I shan't take long.' She's off to pack – at least there is no gang, no band or clan, to tie her down, no brother, cop, no class. Free people here are hard to find, the others talk, they're linked and netted, their virtual friends have all to be apprised, advised, their counsels heard – and all for zero. No one cares if you are here or there. What does it take, to cross that frontier, the cars that circle round at every hour, those strips exposed that snare you as you try to cross? Auto accidents, they say. Motels and gas bars. Carpets on sale that do not fly.

Away, away. Here she comes, packed up already.

I ask Finn, 'How d'you find the hifi lady?'

'Milly? She's near perfect. I talk to her about anything, and she doesn't respond.'

'Careful! She could be a reactionary.'

'OK! I hadn't thought,' he says, 'but yes, she

could be highly trained. And all that gear, her shop. I'll plant my eye in her.'

I say, 'Tania, class warrior – thinks we should each have a little house, like the real workers do. I've just the room I rent from you, and you the room you rent...'

He says, 'The moderns had machines produce the stuff they needed then, the garden sheds and such, to store it in. We posties, postmodernised – we just spin clouds. We don't need space.'

I say, 'I'll tell her so. The quarry guys have written, say – "no charge" if I return their stone pristine, but if it's gouged, they'll sue for everything.'

Finn says wisely, 'Then it's lucky you've nothing, and the rock is sailing round the world. True artists work this way, and never see the millions paid out posthumously.'

'It's not the money that bothers. It's the collectors and enforcers,' I say.

He says, 'That is the lesson – pain of living. If you're dead, a lot of things won't happen to you: debt is one.'

Finn is in his fatigues – 'Off to a funeral. The Colonel, the torturer, at last.'

I say, 'Some kind of respect? I am surprised.'

'To see he's well nailed down, and staked through. And to see who else has come.'

Perry goes with him.

'Perry used to rent to him,' Finn says. 'Goddam her.'

She rents to us too. Rents too, to some guy beneath, who works by night. Comes home and drinks and throws the bottles down, out into the street. There's another rental, seemingly a whore, who's orderly, and over-clean.

'You're the only idlers on my beat,' says Perry. She doesn't joke, we do no neutral service, we're irregulars. Finn's history's complete, and mine all still to come, stored up. Somewhere.

'I pimp for Perry,' Finn says, a little sad, a little proud. 'I book her jobs. She strips – she's satisfied, poor thing, and people like to see old skin. Soft stuff. Her travelled skin, and fingered. That's why the rent is low.'

'I thought she sang?' I say. Finn sublets to me, that's how his room gets paid.

'She rants and moans as she takes off her stuff,' he says.

I tell Tania, 'I never give Finn money. It all goes to Perry. And I always did my art in public spaces, and for free.'

She asks, 'Why did you call that girl a whore? Some hang-up there?'

'She's too clean, always fusses about our dust. Besides, it makes it more romance – sex trade's transgression, not a job. Jazzes life a little up.'

'You're incomprehensible,' she says. 'Not just the words, but what they signify.'

'Come, Tania, we're all spun from the same wool. Don't play this game.'

'Spun from the same sheep, you mean,' she says.

'It's good you won't give up,' I say. 'Saying you don't understand. But it's a bore as well.'

'You need another kissing lesson,' she says.

It comes from the heart, I think. Without fantasy, there'd be little of any of us.

'I've worked for years with these machines,' says Tania, 'so I know all about them. Really, they make affection for them grow. They've to be nursed along, you've to watch out for them. They can get wild, encroach. I do the work, it's not work that they do, just nature and survival. But they produce – I don't. I am their keeper, nothing more. But – other situations, dangers, can arise: there's honour, piracy, resistance to the bad, the good. All ways of widening space. Machinery is not the world, it seems.

'All this I know, but only this. I've nowhere new to go. I've eaten everything, and can't digest. I'm of my time, and every day my time becomes a yesterday. So – boredom. Knowing the tunnels, not digging on.'

I say, 'That's crap, Tania. It's not about you fitting in, it's all about our life here, in Shaky City. Betting the right card, right pill in the right place, right dollar to the right person. That budgie – picking your luck – get it to give you the first nibble. Not changing anything, and changing with everything that comes along, and doing it with great conviction – shave your head, tattoo your bum, or read the Book and praise the banker. It's skills you never knew you had or how you learned them and forgot them too – machines are a bad past, quite the wrong school to go to, quite the wrong facts and rules. Try instead to grab and hold.'

Finn says, 'You'd not believe the stories that I tell you. I've lowdowns on anywhere you've never been, behaviours you can't imagine.'

'I like stories,' I say, 'and they all sound plausible. When you want to stay alive, extreme things must be done and seen. Nothing's too exaggerated, much is never told. What you intend is fanciful, what you achieve is terrible. Best tell it as a story.'

'It seems to me,' says Finn, 'it seems to me' – that's how you start a story, tell a tale. Then the ornament comes in. There's just two landscapes in the world. Or if you like, there's two cellophanes projected on it – one is people and the money that they have or hope to have: money and the things it gets expressed in – white peacocks, diamonds, soldiers to protect you, ladies armed and not. And that's the landscape that the powerful everywhere aspire to, and they frolic in. The other – ideas, the fancy shapes they take, and swirl around, and take odd forms, like clowns or dragons, first loves, plague pits or fields of flowers.'

'It seems quite simple, put like that,' I say. 'But do you, did you, really think like that? Big money or big history? Little deals, or big campaigns? Leaving the bleakly everyday you love, to swim towards the bleak, the other, shore?'

'You can laugh,' says Finn. 'It's the free part of the spectacle.'

He presses on: 'I'll never say real names, people, the countries – the game's still running, play's beginning. Not that it will end! But people – they drop in and out, the actors all swap parts. The freedom fight! I'm not the author, and it's better I don't prompt or hold the book – just take it as a general thing, the situation, adorned, so that for you, for me, it's not a serious thing.'

'Then,' I say, 'what is the point? If it's all for you to hide behind?'

'Ha!' he says, 'that's my strong point. The hiding.'

I ask, 'The Colonel – torturing Algerians?'

'Or Vietnamese, or ... you'd need to check the dates. He could have been a travelling guy, going where the civilisations called.'

I say, 'They have a network, I believe, the torturers. It's the first thing you think of – the after, payments to keep you up.'

Tania says, 'You're funny. You and Finn, both. I

don't mean humorous. Odd. I've never had a funny boyfriend.'

'Ah,' I say. 'You collect?'

'Finn,' she says, 'is Irish.'

'He found the name in a book. A funny book. When you read it, you decide what kind of funny.'

'I'm sure,' she says, 'There's lots of books like that.'

I say to Sophie – the clean woman from downstairs, 'I thought you worked in sex.'

'No,' she says, 'I work nights, the post office. You can't have hang-ups about that.'

'I've no opinion,' I say. 'I know you don't bring people home. But usually I don't, myself.'

We stare at each other. I say, 'It's about finding the meaning. The behaviours, what people let slip when they speak.'

'Meaning,' she says, 'is the big one. Everyone finds one for themselves. But that's not quite what we mean by meaning.'

I'm at a loss, and tell her about Milly. 'Intimacy at irregular intervals, without a word.'

'She may have thought she wouldn't understand you, if she spoke to you. Or vice versa. But she'd a precise idea of when, how much.'

I think of someone saying at a funeral, 'He loved the people.' Maybe it was Lenin's funeral. That was the right time to say a thing like that – the funeral, the meaning we give funerals, the cadaver, and the orator. The ceremony, the loss, exaltation – apprehension. The 'now what?' and 'Now what, Sophie?' I think.

All makes a pattern, so rich and full – I just enjoy the patterns, forms. I suppose the pattern's meaning is itself, its only sense. People don't seem to understand, they want an explanation of the explanation. They want a little piece that fits, and makes a jigsaw picture.

Sophie says, 'I've mail for Finn. I've kept it for him, from him. It's postcards, from those made-up countries, with scripts that don't stand up, but just recline, or hang on wires, like squashed balloons, or bend like rushes in the wind.'

At first I think, 'It's from his past', gestures that don't need response.

'I kept them,' she says. 'I'm the night censor.'

'Seems like you deal with dreams,' I say.

'It's all dreams,' she says.

*

I give the cards to Finn. 'That tart!' he says, 'Keeps it all back.'

He stuffs them in his pocket, like caramels for later.

I realise – Finn doesn't have a past, like we all thought – a history. It's all to come. He fooled us all. The cards – not from the past, but from the future.

He says, 'You must love the people – but not aloud, not till you're dead. Those people, rushing to and fro to cross the bridge – a pitiful sight.'

'But – your medal?' I ask.

'There's those you get when it's all finished, others you get before it starts. Tania got one, I dare say, when she took that awful job, and Milly too. Imagine – to spend a life ...! No wonder Milly can't find anything to say.'

'It's the normal thing,' I say, but know it's not. Maybe it's even better than what's normal.

'Normal's being chased by hippos,' Finn says wisely, and he laughs.

Finn says, 'Tania and Milly both depend on movements quite mechanical – Milly with her waves and spheres, Tania with the wheels and steam, machines that move though bolted to the floor. Watching, watching, them and being sure they never drop a stitch – in total irresponsibility! In olden times, the youngest times, the lover left there on the shore, she screams, she shrieks ...!' – and so he does:

'She knew he'd not be back, maybe some goddess watched him as he died and life will go on in the greys, the underground, or changed into some scuttling thing, a star, a bush,' and Finn again lifts his dark muzzle to the sky, he howls, and wouldn't you, we? – all howl with him, and so do I.

'It's that irregularity,' he says, 'the epic has, and ways of hurting that we've lost.'

Finn says, 'Write them a story. The lives of Milly, Tania, give them some edge, then we'll be off, all four or more.'

And so I write, 'Tania's parents, from a secret service, Russian I believe – they grew their daughter in their secrecy. Was sent to camp, to hunt among the birchtrees, not to kill but to be spotted and be chased – to have the animals race after her, and now she's back with all her friends, and someone has a little radio, and that sweet Moldovan singing, and they comb each others' hair and try to sing along, and then it's night and stars that you don't see any more ... And trails of ants, and flowers that open up just as you touch them, and the crappy food and bread that's not quite right – cheap perfume they all wear and yet gives each a different scent ...'

'Well,' says Finn, 'I guess that will do. She'll have her secret, that's what we want in her. Now – a biog for Milly!'

I write, 'Lots of women, dumb by curse or chance, in opera and in porcelain, and yet expressing...'

'No, no,' says Finn. 'Empty expression will not do! They have to stand distinct, for something you can grasp. You make her seem incapable, and yet she has the gift – to draw you in, not saying anything, and yet decides, commands. I see her as an oracle, high on her smoke. You can't believe their mumbling, oracles – and that's their gift: they say nothing, nothing! But she draws you in, – that cave! – and are those lions behind her throne, or pillows made of smoke?'

'It sounds ideal,' I say, 'but can they both live up to it?'

He pushes his face forward, it almost touches mine, but that would be to lose the focus, and he says, 'We have to sell them. Make them seem important. Maybe anyway they are. Raise expectations. Print their biogs. We can't just travel with some kooky people – we'd just be the usual bunch of spies. We must be valuable, mysterious, people with a secret – not looking for some stuff to steal. So, up our value goes!'

I say, 'Finn – do you still believe people will give you money if you tell them how to leave the money system?'

'Not cash. I don't want it, I'd just pass it on. No good to me, if I can't spend all in an afternoon.'

Where will we end up, I wonder, now that Finn has no past, no history – like me, with just a future. And some postcards.

Will we end where guys just dig and pick some beans and die? Those cities built on trash where all the trade is trash? Jungles where you see the trunks – the pythons – turn into columns of obsidian – the temples big as Galveston, with but a single monk? Or maybe we shall find a window, window of opportunity, where we shall sit and gaze and practise our political skills and sit in circles drinking bottled water ... waiting for the transformation?

'You're puffed up like a frog,' says Tania.

'So's Finn,' I say. 'He has to be, or else he'd not do anything.'

'This froggery,' she says, 'It's quite unlikeable.'

I say, 'It's tragedy, it's civilisation. You make a thing, it stands apart – and it's no longer yours. My stone, – it travels off, it has its non-life, could be hostile. It has neither hair nor shoes.'

She says, 'Your stone again! It's ended up you

don't know where, maybe an object for some cult that's brewing gas to set off in the bus, societies so secret that their secret's lost, bomb blasted with a counter-bomb.'

'Once you've created, off it goes, the stone, the script, you're free of it, and off it sails. Not yours. Until that moment, you're responsible, and after – absolutely not.'

'You haven't answered me at all,' she says.

'I want to go to Bilbao and Surabaya, like the songs say,' I insist.

'I want to go South, where there are sheep and shepherds,' says Finn. 'Once I cut some wire off a lamb's foot. And watch the factories being taken down, and shipped off. Once in the summer, the asylums closed – they call them "protected accommodation" – and they gave the people papers that said "licensed lunatic and beggar", sent them off to wander on foot, alone, in bands. Like the Thirty Years War. And now we're all in bands, and wandering off ...'

Tania drives the car as if it were clouds, maybe those clouds 'high over Ireland', like in the book. Finn's impressed, and says, 'This is your art, Tania, this is your destiny. Just driving us around like we were nabobs.'

Tania's angry and says, 'Go easy on the hetero angle, Finn, watch your mouth or you'll fall into it,' and there floats up an image of the quarry and the people rushing round the walls like panicked words around a mouth.

Milly is there to pick the music, and we go up and down gangplanks to her choice – Tania parking in no space as we boom along – the *Book of Seven Seals*, and Coltrane, and some *Arabella* too – Milly is master of her art, and we sit there, Finn and I, and gaze around like two plump figs awaiting something, on their tree.

'This car is fairly crap,' says Tania, and I say, 'I found it under others – it's a classic, and each door is painted differently so we know who's where to sit, and the trunk holds half a gang, well tied and muffled,' and she sniffs, and says, 'Only you could romance a fucking old Impala,' and she's maybe right.

I'd go by sea, follow my rock, not interested in its sale, but only praise for me.

Finn is for land: he says, 'I'm torn in half. This liberation thing – there's all these guys who want the jobs I'd thought to free them from. Then there are those who want some freedom, but they sit at home and look at little screens and used-car prices, and their work's ephemeral and it doesn't count, it's messages and a button – and who'd want a nation or a state, just look what the big ones do, and all the cities crumbling around the core that's full of tourists with their bottled water – tell me, everyone, what I'm looking for.'

I am stern, I say, 'It seems you didn't found a nation or a state, not like you said, and anyway, that stuff is obsolete or falling down again.'

He grins wolfishly and says, 'Maybe I lied, maybe I exaggerate, but progress is what goes on, and you must snag it with your hook and have it drag you,' and the three of us, we sniff, and look out through the tinted windows that some guy had put in, he must have had a problem for the scene is blurry, it goes by with dusty fields and rusty sheds, and dumps and carts with horses and some guys on elephants in palanquins – all is as normal as it's ever been, and Tania drives us on to boats, then over deserts, monasteries and mosques we see and we're all yawning, and Finn says, 'Let's go to a teadance,' like they had in Budapest, and we all go and disco, stay a day or two, and jiggle up our blood and meet fine people that we never want to see again.

They throw us out and Milly says, 'The art of song is dead,' and we are pleased to hear her talk, and all agree. But liberation, as Finn calls it, still eludes us.

At times we sleep in the vastness of the Impala, dreaming of savannahs, the trek to leave Africa and found civilisations. Sometimes we find hotels or caravanserais. Finn classifies – 'Chickens beneath the bed is character, and in the bed is negligence. Same goes for roosters, unless they're fighting birds.'

The discos in hotels, they go till five, and Finn sleeps in the barn with donkeys, free and rested, till morning when we do our flit.

So, on we go, life's keen observers when the windows give us clarity, and when they cloud up, Finn speaks of freedom, 'freedom with power' – though maybe that's a contradiction since freedom to use power is just a play on words, cosmetic, unless there is some deity around who powers your axe or bullet. 'But,' Finn says, 'freedom without power's just sitting round and playing Snap,' and the space inside the grand old car resounds to talk of Russian counts and German profs who've argued this and that, and Tania says 'hohum', and drives with beauty, never hitting anyone. Milly puts the discs in place, when each one ends she skims it out and hopes some dancing jockey finds it, unwinds each groove and lays it in his heart. Their music binds the troupes of younger nomads as they roam from festival to feast and block our road, but we have destinies more serious and oriented, and we press on, our klaxon sounding softly as we go.

It seems that things have changed and withered, we've passed from centre to the edge – our thoughts and loves and fantasies. There is no centre that is ours, or holds.

Talk passes to the dead. Finn says, 'How do they manage, those Romans? The Romans now, today. Theirs is a squat on skeletons, all those poor houses built on piles of others, collapsed. The new fraudsters – see them rushing through rich palaces, prising off the gilding, trying to start the clocks. All around, it's death, those tall dwellings, attics heaped on attics till the street below is dark, is like death river, full of rain, the cobbles dull as hooded eyes, the crows ...'

I say, 'It's humanity we're supposed to find in death. It puts emotion in you: generous moments, sitting together on the stoup, the dog you've shared and then survives when one of you is gone. Voices, postcards from another life, children that you'll never know, living by some fished-out sea – but there perhaps they have a grasp of past, oil lamps, cod pinned and drying on the barn ...'

'So, on you go,' says Tania. 'I've lots of brothers, the dead ones – gone with a whoosh, like a soldier-guy beside you, as if he's never been, nor told you everything, and "way he goes", a breath as empty as the wind. They're all unique, or think they are, but going – they are all the same. Except,' she pauses, and the car sweeps over the camber, twitches, 'except the special one.'

'What might the special, right, one be?' Finn asks.

'I didn't say "right",' says Tania, heaving the auto

back to its right side: 'The steering's shot. I'll let the auto roll where it must go.'

'Music, voices—' says Milly and Finn interrupts.

'You must say something when it's your turn.'

'They're all encased in darkness,' she says. 'It's their element so they can move around without you seeing them, without falling. Like the stars. All that black to be traversed, and then just gas and molten stuff. The light is just illusion, exception that doesn't fool.'

'Well,' says Finn irritably. 'What does that signify? Of course sound is life, light mere illumination. My family's all dead, just like all yours when you look back – except the few that started me; and all, or nearly, disappear before I do ...'

Maybe Milly wishes she'd kept quiet, but says, 'Just think of all those spaces, Space, where there is no one. Sounds without a point to strike on, no habitation. Breath past, or wires that trembled long ago, lips, fingers vibrating, not a word with sense, or else it's texts, songs stuck to the paper.'

'Well, yes, OK,' says Finn brashly. 'Spend time with the infinite and the chancy, and you're lost. Everything is mediated, and the most concocted – we fool ourselves it's most direct. And probably the thing that we call death is just another of the pauses, not-being has-beens, gone-tomorrows, contacts broken. To complete indifference.' He brushes Milly off, a sign that they've reached intimacy, I feel.

Milly says, 'The silence marinated into every lightless sound – the sound of pride and laughter.

'On, on to Thebes! – the sound of waves receding, hitting no surface, nothing echoes, on and on it goes—'

'Those waves,' Finn cuts in, 'they don't just roll, they break. And there's your music.'

'Yes, Finn,' she says, 'but if they don't?'

Finn says, 'Thebes, yes, let's go to Thebes.'

But Tania says, 'No, no more ships, long seas,' and turns our prow inland. No riddles, and no monsters – all dissolved, resolved. Crumbled up, the roles defaced. No sad destinies.

When we're alone, Finn says to me, 'Milly's all night and dark stars. I like that, it makes me feel quite sunny. It's her territory, like Tania's is driving things and making them seem large. But – that's the way! You start with relics, polish them up – they're gold! Of course.'

'Guy! Suit! Over there!' shouts Finn. We stop. Rich man, maybe politician.

He rides along. He says, 'It's got so complicated – all the agencies, the guys with families, contenting them you have to hire some other guys, and so it grows, and hiring guys you can't remember who ...'

Finn asks, 'And those you can't remember – if they sidle off and find another caesar?'

The guy says, 'Of course, you have to keep them loyal,' and outside we see guys that's playing cards, and shepherds who salute him, lots of sheep, 'But if they sidle off – pum, pum,' and he cocks and fires an imaginary old pistol, and he laughs.

'Really?' and Finn is fascinated, 'It still works? Pum pum, and finding bread and cheese for all those guys, and having them form fours and forties even,' and the guy's amused.

'Oh, many, many more. And in the end you have to have pum pum, but before that there are cops and judges, agencies, the guys that call you. It's a puzzle, but it works!'

Finn says, 'You must get tired,' and now the guy is laughing hard, 'No, no, it's like the rodeo, you have to ride the bull, and while you do, you're up there with the gods. Europe! That's the bull, that's where there's cash. Funny, when you think, a girl screwed by this bull – though with some feisty girls that play along ...' and he nudges Tania.

Finn is satisfied, it works that way, and we are still in Europe, and there's guys in suits all over, probably the world is thus – the pum pum too. Finn is thoughtful, no one has given him their cash despite his wisdom, for a while he spares us theories – the Russians and the Germans, tales of justice and the hands invisible but sure.

'Those hands don't seem invisible,' Tania shouts, and she's tussling with the guy, and Finn explains that systems can't be changed like gears, and she agrees – the motor's hot and stiff.

'Are people giving you their money yet?' Milly asks, and laughs at Finn, who's much annoyed.

We drop the guy, and Tania says, 'That's Rome – it's over there,' a greyish smudge, green stretches, pines, all doing nothing much.

'There's flocks, like in the painted landscapes, centuries ago,' says Finn, excited. 'If you brush two flocks together, some of his may stick to yours. That way you haven't stolen. Though, when you change the marks ... But that's like humans too.'

'Move on, move on,' Tania says.

Milly wonders why the big rich man would wear a suit and go on foot, I tell her it's a part of their religion, always make a pilgrimage dressed good, she says that it's outlandish. Finn keeps saying 'Pum pum', pleased with himself and how the world works out, and maybe he's considering how to free the sheep, or free the shepherds, himself in some important role. And on we drive, and on and on, forgetting about Thebes and Oedipus and that, and Milly's take on destiny – and look like some new *camorristi*, dark glasses every one. Milly's are as black as crow's wings, shaped as such. Quite elegant the four of us, with nowhere much to go, but lean and wicked as we drive, and on and on.

'That was Finn's man on the run,' says Tania, who must know these things. 'Don't be naive, Milly, that's why you wear a suit, to make good photos if they catch you.'

'Well,' says Milly, 'People voted for him, so they've a right to see him spruce.'

'Maybe his voters too are on the run,' says Tania, and indeed we see guys running – some it seems for sport and some from habit, though there's no one after them or interested.

Finn says, 'You guys! The money isn't coming in – and I don't see people to be liberated. Those slaves there, working in the fields – we liberate them now, and they go home to worse things where they came from. Now, the need is on us, our Impala's thirsty, needs some gas and oil, so maybe we should dump it now, before ...'

And so we do, we find a heap of motors and we pile them on our own, and Finn's composed some funeral odes and silently proclaims them, for the memory of mobile times and stuff you threw away, and flowers would grow where you had tossed the junk.

'Time remembered,' says Tania briskly, 'but not experienced,' and it's clear she thinks we're wasters.

I've nostalgia for my rock, I'd like to take a boat, a fast one, dodge the pirates, then ... I say, 'Finn! Suppose my stone gets taken by the pirates! And they ransom it? I can't afford ...' and Milly says a life work's priceless, and when you die some guy will follow on. For me, that does not console, you do it all for fame and praise and gestures, statements, so they say, for whomsoever, and wherever it may end.

The three of them look kindly at me, and they say, 'Of course we'll never leave you, and that rock stays firmly in our sights,' but all have reservations. Finn seeks slaves to free from work or unemployment, Milly wants a step that leads to infinite dark space. Tania would want other brothers, take her for a whirl and end up bad – the world it goes that way, the thing is, never lose the rhythm, and I see that Milly nods: 'the beat', she says.

We could all be painters, standing here, without transport. 'Without brushes too,' says Tania, 'All I can do for you is drive. And Milly here just blocks in shadows. Maybe she could send some music to the spheres, though what they'd do with it's beyond me.'

And now it seems that Finn has some epiphany.

'Not freedom,' he says, 'it's security! Freedom enough to reach security! A status quo it's hard to find but when you do – goddam it, it's so dull! The message is – avoid the epic, armies, scuffles, heroes and heroines – then, what's left? Sufficiency. Not justice and not happiness, not adventure, being brave – or even being risky. Those are qualities you value, not engage with. No history, just the moment clinging and clung on to. I'm finished! I'm done! If I had a home, I'd run to it.'

I say, 'Finn, you're out of time. One foot in history, imperial times – the other shuffling along, the now, not treading in the spills of blood.'

Milly muses, 'What had that guy done?' and Finn says that at least that's life, and running keeps you young, but we don't see the guy again, nor his pursuers, if he has them.

Finn says, 'I've decided, and Milly too, I'm not much interested in sex. That makes a bond between us – even an everlasting one. It leaves more time for lyric bits, the airy arias of life, she calls them.'

'What are these lyric bits?' I ask. 'Though you're well suited.'

'What is more,' says Finn, puffing himself up, 'I find my great objectives are all last century kind. It's slowing down, so I must slow down too. The world. Compassion. Passion too, no doubt. We sing along, but are we on the march? I don't think so. Stealing the rations, selling off the guns – that's what it's all about, and I must come to terms.'

'That's quite sad, Finn,' I say. 'Some of that could make you sleep.'

'There's trouble with your rock,' says Finn. 'I've had a note from Perry – it's impounded. Blasphemy. Said it was a copy of the devil stone. She told them it was grime, at most a cure for peccadilloes, not for sins. Maybe it's loaded up and off again.'

'I should follow it,' I say.

'You wanted to be rid of it,' says Tania.

'Families, brothers, sex too – an age of renunciation. It's in your hand, away it slips. No one will know how we have lived. Without that rock, I'd not know what I'd been.'

'Well,' says Tania. 'It's climbing up the ladders, like it always was.'

Finn pulls a face, and does not speak.

'Let's sit here on the earth outside this bar,' says Milly. 'Inside there's nothing for us, here it's dark, no one will bother us, we'll wear our shades. It's my quiet time with Finn ...'

Finn does not speak, and pulls a face.

*

We sit there on the ground, knowing we're friends as we are parting, and we embrace as best we can and as we feel.

Tania says, 'Helen was just fifteen when it all started,' and we each touch a different thread of destiny, and wander off, each following their purpose. It's ended here, so there is hope it's starting up again elsewhere. Though what it is, we have explored without success.

If we were pilgrims – then, first, Finn's tale, to start it off again. He is backing into history – cool, shady: 'The People! Yes. Perhaps.'

Milly might say. 'My body's white and matt, but I'm tattooed where you can't see, in black, in goth. A life, a body, given to the sounds.'

Tania wants – 'To be Helen. Desired, not loving.'

I – I want to find my rock. Maybe it floats on. I shall find an old ship, be a stoker, drink rum and sweat it out. Turn black as a shovel. Search to find the rock, the marvel.

Finn goes to the fields, lives with the slaves. He says, 'By day, we picked a lot of stuff. And paid protection. After, on our mattresses we lay, and listened each one to our music. There we were free, and resisted some. Then, they would set upon us.'

I say, 'My block, it went to Surabaya, just like in the song. And someone took it, cleaned it down, and it became a pristine four-ton block.'

Finn's maintained by Perry, skimpily, and he has to introduce her act. And Milly says, 'How sad,' she's queen of the night and has a little magic store, she does tattoos and reads the cards, and tells her clients they will die, and charges lots. Alone, inventive in her continent. Siva and Khali – neighbours.

Each is pursuing destiny, but Tania is now far ahead. She drives, and many other things. She's set up as a little boss.

'Those mattresses,' says Finn, 'it brought back Perry in her prime. No one's come to give me money. And I lacked the despair, that drove the other guys. Their basic goodness didn't strike you – not at all. Each had some music, we slept, our ears clogged up with that. Then it was dark, and we got up, and picked some stuff till it was dark again. The money system, slavery itself – both would fall down, before those guys were free to wander off. I fear they're stuck – dead history.'

'It is indeed a sad story, Finn,' I say. 'Maybe there's someone who'll escape and tell it on TV or singing songs.'

'Yes, maybe,' he says. 'They say that art can set you free. But Tania finds that driving motors does the same. I think I need to rethink from the top.'

'You need help to think?' I ask. 'You just leave, and then for you, that's it?'

'Another time? More money. Fewer bandits.

Probably, arms. And ways to use them, with conviction, without hope, without restraint,' he says. 'I hate sects. I hate issues. I hate crowds of people, pushing you, being pushed.'

'That leaves you nowhere,' I say.

'There's lots of us. Marooned. Some have the culture, the old culture – without the substance. Attitude. Fascists of the first hour,' and he makes as if to spit. 'Others, still argumentative. Some, I suppose, are like me.'

'Perry? Selling objects. Art?'

'Who spends thousands on that stuff?'

I think, but do not say, 'Lots do.'

I say, 'I visited, saw Milly, in her booth. Milly, who sees things darkly. Your unlikely double, as we thought, your mate forever – though apparently not.' He's not too interested, but listens. I go on, 'Her bower – it's quite beautiful. A comma in a crowded street, improvised and alien. There's red. And hints of monsters, green and yellow. Crumbling tablets, little pyramids and crystals, she burns them, for a fee. Books of spells. The sacred, the occult, all uncut, unread. A wooden bird that picks out cards. Slits you can look through – take you back, the Cyclades, the churches in the rock, the bloody altars. Childhood. The mystery, the hazard, the transcendental, some lived through, some not – all scumbled up together, a skein of clouds the clients seem to recognise .. Gods that know it all, the snakes and ladders of real lives, that touch of class that's beyond interpretation, but sounds majestic. There's certain groups that recognise the mix, and pay: they recognise fixed destiny, the frog-shaped devil in your shoe, the god omniscient who errs and tells it all to you ... The trouble is, the cops are at her door.'

I tell him how it seems, her India.

'It's true,' says Milly. 'Just like Finn said. People do give you all their money. To get out of the money system. The trouble is, the police say each technique, each myth – is fraud – the cards, the stars, psychology – Thebes, remember?'

I say, 'Forget Thebes, it was about Oedipus. There, they found him out. The fraudster – unaware of what he was. But what is your defence?'

'I tell them none of it is true, that all of it is false, for me. All are fantasy and equal, so I can work with every one. An atheistic pantheon. The trouble is, the other magi, casters of horoscopes and the rest – professionally jealous.'

I say, 'Tania too is out, out of the money system. As boss, she's mostly unconcerned with cash, so long as it comes in ... it's all about the territory, trade, and beating guys and making friends, all that.'

Milly says, 'I thought she was ideal. She drove, you lounged. She chivvied, you spun tales.'

I say, 'These little patterns! Better that they come to nothing. Designs on tablecloths, nothing more.'

I see two cops in black, in oilskin cloaks. They seize poor Milly, bear her up. Away.

Her booth is lofted up, and ends upon a dump.

I see the dump, a-swarm with cops, picking it over – they've driven off the regulars. Black plastic sacks over their uniforms, armed beetles in the stink.

It seems poor Milly's booth was made of notes, the banknotes people gave her. A mulberry, a washed-out brown, purple and bean-green, indigo – the notes curve round her, making so the form, the bower that shielded her, but never gave her luxury, nor yet sufficiency.

Finn asks, 'And did the cops find the wreck, the bower?'

'We have to find poor Milly first,' I say, although the task is awful.

'I fear I can't help,' says Finn, 'Perry is burden enough.'

I say, 'So, then, it's true, behind each social

militant there stands an ageing lady taking off her clothes,' I'm irritated, but I'm not surprised that he's no help.

He does not smile, he says, 'Not just once, she takes them off, the act requires a shift of shapes, from animal to mineral, hamburger into iceberg. Three, four times a night. It must come with the genealogy – the metamorphosis, stuff that she can't grasp.'

He says urgently, without looking at me, 'I'm now convinced – the scene is this. Reproducing capital, oiling it with vanity – it's in the interest of all that it go on. Interest of those who work and those who don't. For it, against it – quite irrelevant. It's the forever system, planetary, what they called the grand design, God's will. Capitalism. It's all there is. It's gravity and light – nature and decoration. Even lumps of stone ... It's brought us down. We're suicides.'

'That sounds like your dying confession, Flinn.'

'It's not made publicly. I'm scouting round for something new, but my, our, big quest is done, and failed. Maybe we should rescue Tania from her bossing? Exciting, whereas Milly's plight is sad and infinite.'

I say, 'Leave Tania out. If she falls, she'll fall through gravity, the force that governs bosses and their molls. Not to be interfered with. Milly, though, is being held until she squawks.'

Finn talks of politics at length. Of sects – it comes

out 'sex' – of entryism into unknown things, of metaphors of wormholes, strings of theory, crossovers from this to that, of brains, of rubber bottles with a single surface, and I think of Milly, those cops, their black capes, like devil birds, lifting her up, bearing her off, to prisons, judgements, unrecorded and unseen. I say,

'We should find Milly, though I hate to offer help, put myself out, and now this seems to be a bore...'

'Tania, though,' Finn says, 'she must know clubs, or even own some,' and his mind is backstage, deep in the patchouli and the pasties, thongs and g-strings, new techniques for stimulating this and satisfying that.

Then, quite unexpectedly he says, 'I must ask Sophie for some guns,' and he is back – with fruitpickers, pastoral and dusty in the sun, and reek of cordite, the running frightened up and down. He says, 'The English have a song – the strawberry fields, a call to revolution or revolt,'

'Sophie must find lots of odd stuff in the post,' I say, 'but, why should she give you guns?'

Finn says, 'Not me – they go to you. And then you give to me. Sophie's job is things like that, and keeping clean. Her contact is with you – and so I'm clean, and by extension, so is she.'

I say, 'But if you're armed, all sides will shoot you down.'

'I have to think it through,' he agrees. 'But if the wretched don't resist, what hope exists for all the rest?'

I search again.

I say, 'I'm looking for Milly.'

Here's a lawyer. Is he a help? Dr Bhindi has a tiger tattooed on the inside of each wrist. One holds a rose, the other a lily in his mouth, one is labelled 'good', the other 'naughty'.

'Don't call me by name,' he says, 'It's confidential.'

I think, 'That sounds perverse.'

'It's very difficult,' he says. 'You don't know where she is. Or how she is. If that is still her name. And does she talk? This means you need the keenest lawyer brain.'

'Yes, yes,' I say, 'Help!'

'It's very difficult,' he says. 'You could try bribes. But who? First, you can pay me, that's a start. Then I might ask some guy.'

'It sounds eternal,' I tell him. I have no cash, so if poor Milly's found, we have to find her money shack. I don't mention this to Bhindi and he pulls his cloth round him like a winding sheet. He looks pitiful. He

stares around. He's Milly, in his mind, and he wants
out. He's shown me photographs of friends and family
– what they tell us to call our 'loved ones' – and they
glare like wolves.

'Where do we start?' he asks, turns up his eyes
until there's only white that shows.

I say, 'You go and look in all the jails.'

'No, no,' he says. 'My name is confidential.'

'Invent one, then,' I say.

'No, no,' he says, 'that is beyond the law.'

'That's where Milly is,' I say.

'No, no,' he says, 'she's deeply in its bosom,' and
he mimes huge breasts, redraws them several times in
air.

I go to all the jails. Three doors – 'criminals, victims,
in-between'. There's a guy here, says, 'My brother –
they speak highly of him.'

I say, 'Dr Bhindi?'

'Of course, my brother.'

We go through the 'in-between' door. I say,
'Milly is somewhere in-between. She doesn't speak.'

The doors lead to the same corridor. There are
three doors – 'condemned, guilty, in-between'. There
is the same corridor, and three doors, 'the pitiful, the

brazen, and the normal'. The corridor is the same –
and so it goes.

The room is big and empty. Dr Bhindi's brother
says, 'No guards. They're at a conference. They don't
like being here. It's the skunk TV. They show us up.
You're not from TV?'

There is a small room, full of women. They all
react, but not all speak.

'Milly, milly, milly,' I say, as if she is a cat. There
is a meowing, Bhindi's brother seems to be collecting
fees. It is an uncomfortable place, quickly, it occurs to
me, I'd die in here.

'Exercise and education,' says Dr Bhindi's
brother. 'Some are learning Sanskrit, some the parallel
bars – but maybe it's too dark to see.'

There is no Milly here – unless she's changed her
name. Or doesn't speak.

'Of course,' Bhindi, my guide, explains, 'there is
a touch of improvisation here – the staff is very keen
on conferences, and making it all tiptop.'

'Your brother,' I ask. 'Can he get people out of
here?'

'There is the law and justice, and all between, that
you might want, and Milly too. It's not like Turkey,
there, you just go in and take your pick – you've seen
the movie? Or Siam – Thailand, they call it now, you
may have seen, and all those movies too. You see, my
friend,' and he breathes close – my, what good meals

he's had – 'Before you start to get a person out, you have to see if that same person's in. You grasp it? A name, a place – those you need to start. Not just some tale of casting spells and houses made of currency.'

'I see,' I say, at a loss.

'And then, of course, there is a set-up fee. That goes to me,' he says.

Dr Bhindi's brothers and his nephews offer a 'searching service' here, in all the jails. First you must pay the fee, and then they ask if street crime is involved, or if it's culture – killings, offence, or cash, or stepping over lines and getting caught. The street crimes are quite casual, indiscriminate, the culture wars are stickier, and to find your prisoner, you need a name to start, a place to put the name. The guards are usually in conferences, but there is talk of Brahmi classes, perhaps beginner Sogdian, and gymnasts on the rings and horse, though it is dark, and maybe you can't see, and you cry Milly, Milly, and there is some laughing and a meowing, but it is quickly over and you scuttle out.

I call Finn, who says, 'The picking season's come. Off to the fields, the wretched and the bounty of the earth! The season's ripe ...'

'Forget it, Finn,' I say, 'you'll just create confusion,' and he says confusion's how it starts and ends, and it is right.

'Of course,' I say, 'I'm with you, Finn, whether you stay or run.'

He takes offence, and there's complaining about Perry and the tenants and I feel whatever happens to him would be his better destiny. And then it strikes me,

'Maybe Tania's friends could intervene. These Dr Bhindis want the cash up front, the dumps are antheaps, with the cops and chancers looking for the bower, the banknotes ... I have done nothing, I can do no more.'

I ask Dr Bhindi's nephew – or maybe it was the doctor himself – 'Dr Bhindi is a lawyer?'

'What? Dr Bhindi is inspector of corrections. He will show you only the best jails, the very best.'

'I thought – rights, all that ...'

Bhindi replies, 'Who better than the chief inspector? This Milly – where's she from?'

I say, blindly, 'The hifi shop.'

'Aha. A spy.'

'Possibly,' I try again, and raise my stake, 'From Thebes.'

'Theebz,' says Dr Bhindi carefully. 'If I were her, I'd keep quiet myself, not speak. A dreadful place, a funny name – we did it all at school. Murder and incest. Hmmm – bad boys jail for that.'

He tries many times, 'Thebes', poking out his brown-green tongue to penetrate the opening of the city.

I say, 'Only one guy, who didn't know ...'

The doctor says, 'Ignorance of the law is no excuse. This "Milly" – could she be a mother figure? Too much sex within the family can clam you up. Then, there's the sphinx! That could be her, and I recall there is another epic, running from war to massacre, some minor shapeshifting on the way, to cover up some sex with – pigs.' He shows disgust, and says, 'Of course, I'm not a pigophobe like some guys here. Their problem lies with monotheism, Mongols from the badlands, tearing down the stuff we indigenes threw up. And so, they dump it all on pigs. But epics – do you know, some of ours can last for months, and once you start you cannot stop, we know them all by heart, it's bad luck if you interrupt your recitation, to eat or sleep,' and he looks at me accusingly.

I say, 'Milly – she did a service, that is all – the science, like you guys do, then the magic – and I see you on your break, going to booths for spells and horoscopes – so, what's the harm?'

'The harm, my friend,' says Dr Bhindi, kindly, holding my arms and pushing me into the street, 'lies in your *habeas corpus*. Since we have no body, you can't do a deal. But,' and he points to the steaming dump that looms above the city, 'find the money house. Then we can talk.'

He pauses, then, a confidence: 'There's lots here have a money house. It's quite the thing, it's called professional service, and the public good. From one money house,' he intones, 'there spring a hundred, by reproduction virginal – it's all been sorted out in epic form. First the poetry, then the real. I know it all – the silent woman, who then disappears – divinity of luck and fortune. Consider her,' and he pauses, the judgment arrives, is final, 'a benefactress. And as she disappears, a hail of golden coins, an interlude of animals that speak. Now you can go, my friend, in all tranquillity.'

The Bhindi episode concludes.

'I never bother about surnames,' says Finn, 'so I can't help with Milly. I expect she wanted to disappear.'

'Wanting or not,' I say, 'she has, completely. No memorial.'

'That's the way it is now,' says Finn wisely, 'if you want some action, and don't have a big building behind you.'

'And an office,' I add, hoping to hurry things along.

'The real movers don't have an office, they hop from Fred's to Ted's. Same with names, passports. The lowest dogs have lots of them, but the real hunters – just two or three, with good clean nationalities. No dreg nations. Sophie knows – she sees the stamps. Did you know, she can't steam them off any more? That really cuts down the interest, and the inflow.'

'How do you know all these plausible things?' I ask him.

He talks long about himself. His moral commitment to the right sides, deploring excess and failure. His own modest part as counsellor and drinking pal of this big cheese, that bright poppy and their wives and mistresses.

'Did you really expect you were liberating huddled masses?' I ask.

He is solemn, 'Certainly – everyone has, and everyone needs, some values that he, she, believes in quite sincerely. It's not teddy bears, you know – you have to be scared all the time, not just at picnic time, when they boil up the pot and tip you in. If you're not scared – then what's the point? You must believe, make your analyses! And come for you they will, for years and years – and so, it's best to have a certainty, who are your friends, your enemies.'

'So, it's movieland for ever?' I ask. 'But what exactly did you do – not scared in foxholes, I should bet, but seeking out the foxes at the head?'

'I'm telling you all secrets. Things you've never heard,' he says and rubs his nose, as if it's running confidences.

'Put like that, what you have done, well – it could be rather boring.'

He's offended, or pretends to be. He's changed the absent Milly from tragedy to minor spy. He concludes, 'You want to make a mark, and that's quite human. Don't go on patrol, don't go in an armoured truck, don't stand where some guy falls on you, and don't wear woolly socks. Don't attract the bad stuff, but defend the right.'

I'm not impressed. I say, 'The pickers? Guns for the pickers, where does that come in?'

'It's the Zeitgeist! Everyone must do some action, bankers see the pyramids slide down, and sitting in the park – wow! there's a bomb, and who is that and who was sitting there, and bodies – is this one or three...? You know the scene. So, you don't want to end, a pair of severed legs without a name – nor to pretend your banging up and down some intricate land will bring bright light and friends. No! You want to turn that screw, the screw that holds the water in, or lets it out. You need to be the guy that really does the strategy, and doesn't talk, or puff. Like Milly.'

I say, 'You knew her better – she didn't seem to me like that.'

He says, 'We'll say no more. But I observe, you

don't know people very well. Tania now – a power behind the slot machines. Milly, no doubt, her mission going on – like they say, an epic takes some months to tell, and you can't interrupt it.'

I say, 'I just recall that random wordless kissing. But yes, those epics, once you start you mustn't stop,' and I think of the railway carriages, people mumbling through a million lines, eating through a straw and cursing someone who has started them – they mustn't stop, they have to reach the end.

'That's very important,' says Finn: 'To have an end.'

'It was the Battle of Tumbledown,' says Finn.

'Where are you, Finn?'

'I think it better to go on picking – you can pick your way over the continent, tomatoes, grapes, then the heavy stuff – potatoes specially, by luck, there's no machines. Then battle, well, it was running lots, then lying low, then running more.'

'That's to your liking, Finn,' I say. I do not tell him of my luck, if luck it is. Nor of Milly's fate, her challenges to fate and destiny which ended bad – it seems. Unless ... she did a deal, and Dr Bhindi and his clan have shared the loot and she is off, foretelling bad ends to paying customers.

I think of Milly in her cell – the awful solitude, the awful company, white time that passes over like a broom of thorns, and makes your memory strip and strip until there's nothing left but memory, and true and false have disappeared and every moment's empty and it scratches on, there you have nothing left to pick but promises and fighting for some stuff that could be eat or drink, and you don't need it but you have to raven down because to die is deader still than what you are ... and so I muse, and say to Finn, 'It may be Milly's in a place where there's no metamorphosis.'

'And maybe she is not,' he says. 'At least I'm rid of Perry, and I'm lying low. The guys – well, some were seeing witches everywhere, and frightened of the light, the dark. They came from places so remote they're left blank on the maps – saints and magicians, executioners – in equal numbers. Then there were the monotheists, various kinds, and pretty strict with me and hostile too. And hate and hope they hopped around, you never knew, and arguing like monks for this and that. The lot of each was just the same, but it was destiny we talked about, a lot of here and now, and then, and later still.'

'That doesn't sound your scene at all.'

'Then there were Sophie's guns, supposed to sharpen up the sides, so when the bandits came, and then the cops – and they were after us – we could defend, at least provoke. But Sophie had a plan.'

I say, 'Sophie tells me, "Finn, your friend, he made a terrible mess."'

'Yes,' Finn says, 'I messed up both our plans. The cops should take the terrorists, whoever they might be, believers indiscriminately expelled, and those that were left – sign on for work eternal in the fields. But in the end, they fired at us, at all of us, at all the sides, from every side, and so we ran and ran, all ran, and here I am, the others all dispersed, and picking somewhere else.'

'Milly's lost,' I tell Tania.

'Just because you can't find her doesn't mean she's lost,' she says.

'Finn is taken up with things,' I say.

'I couldn't give him guns – he wanted to be found out, I'd not have told. It's all a strategem.'

'Why are guns the latest thing?' I ask.

'All the professionals need them – it's the only way to work, after everything fell down,' she says.

'Like that bridge? But almost everyone is still alive,' I say.

'He wanted to make history, and love the people, when he's dead. But that has fallen down as well.'

'Maybe your boss can help with Milly,' I say, 'And do you call him boss in bed?'

'I'm still the driver,' Tania says, and laughs.

'The country where poor Milly is,' I say. 'It's knitted up, everybody has a place, though some eat dirt and some eat gold, and some don't seem to eat at all. So, somewhere there's a place for her. Just find it. Avoid – if you are able – a contact with the Dr Bhindis.'

Tania stares at me – 'Yes, I remember, you and I, we once were lovers. Goodness, but that's strange.'

She says, 'The silent one – if she's alive, is living in a definite place ... she's safe so long as they don't find the money house – but then she'd be exposed, if someone thinks it is still hers. If she's not already gone, that is the moment when she really disappears,' and she pauses, her tongue just lingering out, as if a puzzle has been solved.

'You fucking bourgeois,' says Tania. 'All the obstacles put in our way. Pushed to the edge, and then you call us bandits.'

I'm not impressed. I say, 'All I want is for your bandits to contact the other bandits, get Milly out, let her foretell disaster in her usual way, and we'll forget it all.'

'It's just a little thing,' she says. 'And no. No, absolutely not.'

Wars go on, people are swept away, the billions wobble, economy founders, all that.

I say, 'Finn and I don't have much economy,' and Tania's pushing, driving hard.

'Behind you both is Perry,' she says, 'ridden by some famous names and now high mistress of the market – art or skin.'

'She's a performance artist,' I say. 'Nothing more. I don't judge. Are we on to justice and equality yet? It's like those three bells in your machines – they don't come up because it's all glued up inside ....'

'You're just a heap of bones inside a heap of clothes,' she insists.

I agree that even Perry is more lithe and wholesome and I say, 'I want to smooth this irritation out, and go on to the next.'

Tania starts again, right from the top, and adds, 'The quarry, people going down all arms and legs, what mattered to you was your rock, and nothing else.'

'No, no,' I say. 'The rock plus what was to be sculpted into it – that was what mattered.'

'Pfat,' a spit more powerful than a spit itself. I try:

'I love you. Tania,' but it doesn't work, nor humanism, seeking the lost, it doesn't interrupt her rush.

'You're quite pathetic,' she says, and I think maybe I'll tell the cops about it all, but then, they surely know it now, so why ....

'I like your gilet, Tania,' I say.

'You're right,' she says. 'It's me. Well done.'

And so, I go to work for Tania, Boss.

Finn goes to pick – tomatoes, peppers, eggplants, stuff on the ground and in the air, and stuff that comes by truck at night.

Tania says, 'I've quite a corporation here, with all the pros that help.'

I say, 'Just let me take the oath, the sacred picture burning in my palm, but – no conferences, and no weekend bonding. Please.'

'So be it,' Tania says. 'Drugs is infantile, but the cops say it brings fortunes, so everyone wants in. I'm for the growers of the stuff – but life is cruel, and I'm exceptional, like you and Finn, although we maybe see things different.'

I have a call from Finn, I tell him all.

'Tania's our rock, it's true,' he says and laughs. 'Between the bandits and the cops, the choice is not an easy one – it's slavery or expulsion, for my guys. I hope to stir things up, and run ....'

'Not public opinion, Finn!' I say. 'Surely you've learned ...'

He's offended and says, 'I'm not your Sundance Kid – I want to live, and live again. But you

– you'll find a spot you think is clean, but you're in there with all the rest, a corporate stooge ...'

Then I'm offended. 'That's all a hundred years ago,' I say. 'Now, everyone's cut in. As Tania says, the bankers, lawyers, presidents and priests – who doesn't want their piece? Sometimes it's fear that keeps them quiet, but still they buy the drugs and whores, bring in the wretched of the earth or keep them out, and watch them sweat, and buy the clothes they make and all that stuff that they keep cheap ...'

Finn sniffs dismissively. 'You know it but you bow before it. Maybe you even vote?'

I say, 'I could have gone on fiddling with my rock...'

'But you globalised it when I mocked you.'

We stare at each other, and I wish I was with Finn, adventure, wonder who he'll give his guns to, when he'll run away, and when that Sophie'll make her call and bring the curtain down.

Tania tells me. 'You'll settle the accounts with our dishonest friends. It's saddening, how they turn against me. You prick their thumbs, you burn the sacred pictures in their palms – and still they steal from me.'

I flourish in the job. Justice I bring, and retribution.

'Let your gay side out too,' says Tania. Screwing the boss, or else the boss's girl, it's quite the classic scene, banal but pleasant too, and better than the fields of aubergine that Finn must clear.

We celebrate one evening with the President. I'm at my stones, my rocks again, my art. My clothes are outré, but they're Tania's choice. Forget poor Milly, nothing's done.

I tell the guy, 'I'm up to ten-ton marbles now.'

He says they'll buy them for some park: – 'Don't make them square, for fear it hurts the kids,' he says, and shows he's thoughtful, here come pics of him, astride white horses, rhinos and the like, and maybe riding women too that he's been gifted, and when we eat there's live crabs crawling on the cloth with caviar and stuff that's ladled on their backs, and as they pass you take your pick, and after, they are all boiled up. Then off he goes to bed, selecting three or four – the feistier guests – and then the rest of us take to our carriages, and feel we've been affiliated to something big and thrusting on.

And Tania says, 'Don't you recall, the book, it tells us how "we see, we hear, we conceive, of the world in a lopsided fashion" and how "Odette is in Swann's eyes a difficult woman to conquer" – it brings it back, those thrilling days, those sexy birds! Here is the President, our Swann, and that Albanian girl. She must be Leda. No doubt she's tough. More than just enjoyment for those two – they must be epic ... Really, it's all history, forged before our eyes. They are tremendous beasts, and all for our delight. But why "lopsided"? It's not lopsided, what I see.'

I ask, 'Did you memorise all those books?'

'You told me – seek out funny books – these are the tops!' she says .'And yes, I do recall them all, and in the train repeat them to myself, you start right from the head and cannot stop until the end, if end there is. Maybe it's all there, that writer guy, he talks of a "dimension of Time", hard to escape that one.'

I agree. We both feel we have been blessed, anointed somehow on our brows, though I tell Tania, 'Books slip away, not like my rocks,' and then I think of other guys in slower trains, a-mumbling through the deeds of gods and monkeys, heroes all, but Tania is our rock, a stone with soul that's fixed and polished.

'That lover stuff, the "us",' she says. 'Go light on that.'

I call Finn, tell him, 'Change your name. Come home. I manage Perry now – but she's always yours, your last resort. Where are you, Finn?'

He says, 'A middling town. I see the road encircling it from here. You take the train, it goes to bigger towns. The road, it's not for crossing, that belt that keeps the people in.'

'You sound sour, Finn,' I say. '"On the run" no longer suits?'

'There's a bar here.' he says. 'They dance old style. Remember – *apache*? – we're mostly men, it doesn't count. Ceramic ashtrays. I'm quite at home.'

I say, 'We're not done yet, Finn,' and there is no reply.

Tania says, 'They're opening the China branch.'

'Shall we drive there? I'm curious about Lanzhou.'

'No, no, we're here and stay,' she says.

'That means the branch is us. Taken in and taken over. And will our boss come to the feast? There must be one ...'

'There's always bosses,' she replies.

'You never answer questions. So, how do you want things set up?'

She looks prim. 'Some folklore. No women available or for sale. Wine.'

I ask, 'Where's the wine from?'

'It's ours. We get it off that little screen,' she says. There's many crates. The label is handwritten, FINN FECIT: FINN IS. It tastes sour.

Fireworks and clowns, crisps in celadon bowls, lanterns – a parade of dogs.

'It's quite characteristic,' I say to please her.

'It's quite unnecessary,' she says. 'They know it all. They're local.'

It does not end well. Though, it doesn't end at all. Perhaps for Milly, and for Finn, it does.

We're in the car, Tania is driving and we waft along. She is the artist, and we're back to machines, and some of us are back to breaking shins, and others picking grapes and bottling. Milly saw it all, that's why she didn't speak, and clung and hugged.

I say, and sing, '"Goodbye, goodbye, my summer and my time is up" and it is done ...' and Tania says that nothing's done, and we can't afford nostalgia, our work is never finished, it's all manual.

To us, bad things won't happen, and the pressing fear of death – it's quite exaggerated, so Tania says.

Then we see the car behind.

'Go in that gap,' I say, and so she goes, we suck our cheeks in, and we pass. We're nearly home. The other car is plumper, hits my ten-ton block, the marble starts to shatter, we'll have no memorial – nor will this guy, he's terribly dispersed, though there'll be others after him, and after us! – maybe better drivers and with leaner cars.

Tania says, 'It could be that Chinese guy,' and she wonders what he wanted.

I ask, 'So are we on the run?'

She's quite moved, and says, 'It's what we're made for, how we're trained – not to end like Milly, all that cash that we can't spend.'

'It isn't about money,' I say. 'We've left the

money system far behind – it's territory now, and giving orders to the guys.'

She agrees, we are at one, and almost friendly, and she says, 'We're safe, we're safe at last. This is the destiny.'

I don't understand, but I agree and say, 'We're safe. And powerful too.'

THE SEA

Merd'! V'là l'hiver et ses dur'tés,
V'là l'moment de n' pus s' mettre à poils:
V'là qu' ceuss' qui tienn'nt la queue d' la poêle
 Dans l'midi vont s' carapater!
            Jehan Rictus, *Les soliloques du pauvre*

The Owl and the Pussy-cat went to sea
                            Edward Lear

'Your lot's been killing Afghans again,' I say. 'Not my lot,' she says. ' Besides, think of the good it brings their women.'

I say, 'If I killed everyone with old thoughts, the only one left is me, and only half of me at that.'

Ancient Egypt. What a show!

We look at the exhibits, some pharoah's chariot, like the carts they sell kvass from. Lots of dead here too.

She says, 'I don't like the colours.'

I say, 'Just because we're in a show, not yobbing on the beach, you don't need say silly things to show you were at school.'

Black, gold, a red like canned meat, pale scrollings like cats' tails. Faded, from being underground.

I spent all my money on a pad, right in the city's heart. I love the scene of cop cars, druggies and their druggy friends, skirmishes by night, the trumpets flourishing, the boring afternoons. It fires me up. But – the money's spent, the credit too, and so we've nothing left.

If I die now, today, at twelve o'clock, I die rich and well-regarded.

She says, 'Thinking well of yourself – that's what gives good reputation to the world, the stars, us.'

I say, 'Exactly. It should make you glad. If I'm thinking badly of myself, the lot can collapse into

171

itself, a black buzz for all I care. Then where'd you be?'

She says, 'You're a snob, about yourself! You snob your narcissism!'

How true, how silly.

We're shouting on the road edge, though we could be shouting anywhere, concentrating like we're illuminating manuscripts. The text starts: 'In the beginning was the word, an argument, a crackup.'

I shove her gently.

It's exciting, and I calculate the drop. Regret. Down she's gone, and out of sight. These rifts, clefts in the rock, they go down thirty metres. Or two. Full of treelets, stuff to hold to, or that rips you.

Silence. How delightful. How awful. You bet a fortune on a horse to lose. And if it wins? If she's dead – for me, justice will come, and will be done. If she lives – I'm off my hook. And back she'll come.

If I'd died a minute ago, I'd have died rich. Then, she'd be living rich. Now, five after twelve, I'm a poor murderer on the run, and she is dead. If she is. Nature is witty? No, can't even take a joke, let alone tell one. The wit – is me! I'd better run, before she scrambles out. Or doesn't.

At the level of the clouds, all is serene, and caused by large things that multiply and feed – the causes. They don't go away. Can't ignore a single one. So, here comes the drought, the flood, and then the famine and calamity. All complexly, rationally, caused by chains of things, events, chances that aren't really chance – not as a will, and not as reason, but in their combination – it all becomes absolutely reason.

Then, at the bottom level – us – there is the chaos, pure chance, the unforeseeable, the bad luck, evil eyes, the warrior's heel that's stabbed – by pure chance. Or malice. Or revenge. Justice must come.

There you are, hut in the forest, chasing the wild pig, eating the root – and there's your neighbour, slaughtered. You've escaped: you weren't at home. The first car skids and skates, survives – yours hits the tree – this time, the big kebab is you.

In my case, though, her murder seems quite different. No big causes that I can see – unless it's family, genetics, civilisation, love, all that – behind an act, precise, of shove and run. The consequences are material – but I've no idea what they might be. We unlucky ones – we never know who suffers from our vote, directive, bomb that's full of leaflets – or of primal matter sounded off. It leaves us free: to practise repentance or indifference. Philosophy.

The killing of the one we love, or are indifferent to – here is the basis of our law, our destiny, our quest for leaving marks, improving on design: the 'is' we're tumbled into.

It doesn't seem to mean all this to me, here, in this minute, and the next.

I can't run any more. There's no one following, and so I walk, quite fast. These trees, so high – someone has marked them with a saw – condemned or spared? The woodman knows – and there's a woodbird, tells it all, over and over. 'Woodman, woodman, spare that tree ...' the song, the human one: you can't keep it out. I sing it, shout it, till the bird flaps off, finds a new perch and silent waits to see if it's invaded some new territory.

The city – where the early snow sifts like salt over the sidewalks: frozen slush is black and white, the shoe-heels have made it bottlebottoms. It's all Dickens, ladies with furry coats, the cruisers with one red eye, their cops looking for some eats, grazing slowly up and down the storefronts, and there's sweets, candies, red and green like lumps of plastic or the glass fused you find in smelter's tailings.

This is where the ornament is all American, the history too, suburbs and trashcans, automobiles – but it's not all assimilated, not united states – won't ever be here, because of different language, more important than the similar of fusty pastorals of province. Here, yes, there's fisheries and deserts, endless ruts for lakes, expanses of unpainted canvas, just white, snow no one's bothered with, no tracks, no people. It's a world quite rich, a 'Canada' where there's everything, and airy palaces without feet and shoes and socks that link them to the earth, to us. There's some guys here that seek the earth, and others pleased that cities don't have any; lots of space and spaces between people – grand space, it doesn't impinge, except as weather, and there's no green or brown, just a fauvist show in fall.

My feet take up the beat, I rock it – 'Put down that forest razor ...' and voice, shoes, and me, we all prance along, a quick parade step, I put in the goosey bit and up the arms go, shoulder height. I'm singing along, that I'm ex-hilarated, ex- what else? –onerated, -tenuated, -terminated, ex -iled. That covers it all. Here there's houses – some guy in a car hits a cat – it runs, notwithstanding, they find a refuge always, then look see if they're hurt.

The guy's surrounded by the crowd, he says, 'Fucking cat's own fault,' and I lift a hunk of rock and thrust it in his face:

'So, this is your fault as well,' I say. I'm all afire, and justice is the sentiment that runs through me and all these other guys. We stand off for a while, then it's the usual clash of shields, stamp feet, and off we go again, forgetting, and the song goes on, how the tree protected the guy from his wife, and it gets closer to me, 'It has oft protected me, and I'll protect it now.'

Touch not a single bough.

That's how it should be: ritual and manners, softening the thrust.

This place is full of cadavers, waiting just below the crust, popping up, reminders. An entertainment, memento mori – or just to show how hard it is to stow them all away unseen, the clay, they call us, every plate and cup is made of clay, fingers turned to clay – no need to wash it off.

They'll not find her for a thousand years, then, as a skeleton and nameless, there in the bed alongside, it's not a thought than resonates, inspires. Crawling out she comes, that headrock – skullbone – bigger than the rest that's just a bunch of twigs. The empty head, though...all that dentistry gone to waste, the brain too, disappeared, all borne off somewhere.

Thinking on, 'Woodman, woodman ... spare,' and I skeeter off, away from the city, through the villagers, and conclude the episode.

Unintended effects? or just the usual actions, starting out on castaway journeys? Not house of the dead for me, perhaps a house of near death, after death. Or death avoided!

Those guys in the bus are staring at me, they

could be angels of vengeance, or thieves. Perhaps it's my space they want? Get off, and walk again.

This guy here, sat on this bench, could know lots I've never known, or have forgotten – Freud, the Barberini faun, Turandot ...

Of course, I confess.

He says, 'You pushed her? for the boring things she said? love of your life? You scum.'

'No love, no hatred,' I say, 'But, of course I'm scum. It's unconfessable. Or unpardonable. It's the consequences that haunt you – those are the dead and everlasting things: the act itself, it's all just elbow.'

'That's no excuse,' he says, as if I'd looked for one.

It seems he's some kind of top cop, way above mere murders – philosophy and the globe, is what he's responsible for. A colonel, at the least. He confides in me: 'Yes, at first, we Americans, they ...'

'Americans?' I interrupt. 'Anomalous, a bit old hat, don't you think?' and he stares at me, then goes on, 'At first they want to be Romans, conquering. Those awful paintings. Mad emperors, bad sex, and slaughter of fine animals. All with insouciance. Maybe a touch of the journey to Cythère.' He pauses, to see if I'm catching up. He goes on, 'You know, old boys in kilts – rifles, flushing prey, banging it down. That did for South America. Then, they had a meeting – I was there. They were still Romans, but the empire'd split, like an amoeba.

'"It's all just nationalism," they said. "The guys that don't like us. There's no idea behind it and no conspiracy. See them make command economies, then – if all goes well for them they'll make a middle class that's just like ours. If it goes bad, the army runs it for a while, and then we start again. Selling them stuff."'

I feel it sounds familiar, but the people and the places don't spring out, connect.

He goes on, 'Then, they had another meeting – yes, me too – "First," they said, "Lay states: with lots of arms, but weakened by a parliament, with space for us, the graft, those licences. They'll be our protectorates. There's no idea behind it, there's some terrorists, but well, they can be contained: it's all a muddle, politics together with the good and simple life, all bundled up, a bid for holy ghostly power. Our friends, a row of nesting boxes, some mad guys, is all. We've had our own conversion ramps – rebirth, death tucked in the freezer – the world is closing down, better to close it soon, before it falls. And so, we'll push our frontier out, and maybe find some more barbarians to civilise and sell them stuff, and arms that aren't as good as ours – can't be too careful there, you know – and so we'll trade and make our deals, but still be top."

'Then, they're Romans once again, and now they – we – can't do the trading, and there's mad guys that's terrorists and other guys that may be mad but also aren't too good at running things. And so, we set up stalls all over, but the stuff's no longer ours, and so we think of where to pitch the frontier – and it's still way out, but lot's been given up. Then there's what some call religion, it's all everywhere. And other guys are starting up, but they don't have a Rome – they see there's no idea, not here nor there, just administering of things – and that is History, my friend. Paints with a wide brush, and doesn't think too hard of where it puts the colour, draws the lines.'

I say, 'It's falling down all round – and you guys is struggling still to be on top, and other guys are beating you, and still it all falls down. One world – and lots of guys still battling on against ...'

He interrupts, 'Against, or maybe for. Not enough Romans to go round. The friend we have is India, the ally, and the foe we'll fight is China. The little wars that we don't win – it's just rehearsal, then the big one comes. In between – all's dark and strange, a world of past and passing things. and no idea. No big idea. How does that seem to you?'

I say, 'There's not much there that I can take away. Are you recruiting me? Those lines and matchstick figures – not much room for heroes in that stew. And India! It's all a box of magic! What friendship's there?'

He looks into an empty distance. I think he

doesn't know.

'I know,' he says. 'It's your wife all over. There she is, the bright and flighty girl, she wears a yellow dress, who knows? and who remembers? some smart remark from her, and off you go. Off your head you go! Love, passion, all the complicated maze of this and that, the poems half forgotten, relatives you never meet, friends to avoid – we've all been there – and then, it's all smudged out. You know, I know – it's irritation! Blots it out – the joy, abandon. A little push, and you are out, over the wall, the civilisation. New loves may come, you fear, more quests and tests. But for the now – it's done! Irritation. Self-defence. Thus far, you say – and so, screw you, down in the rock you go! And so, it's war, or something like.'

I say, 'You'd call it victory, put like that.'

He smiles slyly, 'If they find a body, you'll be in a long story.'

I've suffered America in history. Now, my wife, down in the hole.

'You – they – don't make any sense,' I say.

'It doesn't have to,' he says. 'It's strategy.'

'You set up fences bound to be knocked down,' I say.

'Yes,' he says, 'but we'll be far away. And when everywhere except your home is left a desert – then you've won. It was ever so. The woman you pushed down – same thing. Annoyance: not putting up with, that's how the whole thing moves.'

'You may be right,' I say, 'and is that strategy?'

'There's millions of us,' the guy laughs, 'each with his say. We're Romans. Some just scratch on tiles, some watch ostriches decapitated, and others scribble, scribble. That is life, my friend. Not death, like yours.'

'You're right,' I say. 'The thing is not to bear a grudge, to set the positive on its stand, forget the rest. The bad things, happening in the night.'

So, here's another spy that's set to wander through the world, he offers me the bottle, takes a slug to show it's clean, and says, 'Manhattans. They take quick revenge,' and laughs again.

'What the fuck, in any case,' he says, now we are friends and confidants, 'is a woman-killer doing, giving me a lesson on politics?'

'It didn't seem so inappropriate,' I say. 'Besides the doubts that enter in, unasked, diminished this and that, prevision, motives – it's all part of the journey to extinction we're all making – so, what's your beef?'

The Remembering. Love. That chemical broth, sex – always good. Or often not – entwined with love, one kind of it, though other kinds are often just not there ... love of country, place, unknown families and fathers. Love abandoned, too – the multiple thyroids playing up or silent, motors running on a coupla plugs. Superior sorts of love, good sex, yes! – but that is dwindling out, though soon replaced by something else. Devotion, they say, like religion: into that church, that mosque, on hands and knees, gentlemen remove their shoes – receive the eternal answer to the unasked question. Answers galore, indeed, each waiting in the outfield, ready to run, maybe never called upon, rooted like scarecrows in left field. Waiting for the challenge. Sure pair of hands, religion, always there, want it or not, even with reason added, running on, a horseless buggy. Notwithstanding. Nevertheless – even when you're not there, down the road it trundles.

The guy says, 'She must have found you difficult.'

'You must attack the block,' I say. 'What's difficult is just the skin. It's like the surgeon says, 'I'm in.' But why'd she want to be a surgeon, get inside? The inside's the same in everyone, but you need a special skin to work that out, because they look all the same, insides. It's the skin that's different, and difficult.'

The guy's bored, but convinced. 'You have no place,' he says, 'and no possessions. No parents – childhood's an idea that bounces off. No schooling visible. Class – a conundrum. Politics – a postcard pacifism, lots of hate and surface. Some scrappy faith in love that's lost, in death to come, and sex irregular. You are the perfect guy we want. You've the thing that turns you into gold, with fittings of titanium. A murder! A botched killing, or an exasperated elbow.'

'You don't want me,' I say, 'I tox you up. I tox up everyone, it gives me drift, it points me to a goal.'

'On, on, go on!' He's delighted: 'Your music! The spiritual life without a spirit, the ecstasy without a pill, without epiphany. I see you in your nowhere room, I see you make an omelette, there! you throw some beans on top, you are on a second bottle of Dubonnet, brandy to follow – you're not drunk, the stuff just drops inside and makes more melancholy. You are one of us.'

'I'll make an offer,' says the guy, holding my secret in his fingertips, like a serpent's egg. 'You'll be a Forest Ranger. You like forests, no? A resource they are, if dangerous.'

I say, 'Really, I'm on the other side. I'm not with you, your lot.'

He says, 'There is no other side. Now, it's back to countries and religions. Back to the nursery. Back we go.'

I stare at him: 'It's all burnt down, and out. That's why they run. Their life is eaten up.' Then,

'The other Rangers?' I ask.

'Imagine there are none. You'll have it to yourself, the forest, though there are guys that sleep in it, they give no bother – watch out for the bands, though, and the fires. Money you'll have in sacks.'

We think it over.

'And are there stores to spend it in?' I ask.

'Naturally not. You'll eat the animals when there's need. And virtuously save.'

I think, if there is another side, I'm on it, but I'm in the trap. 'What shall I do?' I ask.

'We'll see you as a sleeper, ours: and then we'll call. Just the sly ambitious type we need. You wasted that pure girl, you know – too bad for you, and good for us. I wonder,' and he stares. 'What do the pure think, all the time! They must have marble brains, that dazzle with the light, as you peek in.'

The lady vanished – it's just convention, though for her there's meaning, I suppose. And now there's meaning, some of hers, for me.

But, ah, the forest, my appanage, the place where you repent and search – here is the stock of animals, one behind each tree, timid, aggressive. Just caught in passing, in the image. It's not epiphany, not yet, it is the book with seals unbroken, the body not yet penetrated, the climate not yet shaken, the map without a feature.

Quite untended. Here, my feet push up against me, the sprung forest floor – here's branches, fallen needles, great mushrooms never seen the sun, they grow a span across, like stepping stones here in the stream, and there are veins of tiny rivers, paths the bears have made, layered with spilled fruit – and here a clearing where all the paths and waters rise. Empty, open like a theatre – an audience for sure will come, some play be acted out, the clouds will skim across the stars and we shall see by moonlight.

'We', I thought 'we'. I'm sure there's others here, at least their shoulders, knees, I feel their presence, though there's little we can say, communicate. The days and nights, those are our Time, the light, the dark – the answers and the questions. These don't concern the others, guys lounging in the grass.

The forest is a sacred body, and I feel myself its eye, the breath, the beating thing that wafts through all, that sees, that ventilates, that sets the rhythm: giant and numen – and I say to him, the spy,

'OK. I'll do it, for your silence. You know what and why. It's understood – I'm not on your side – not ever.'

'Just as you wish,' he says. 'We'll leave the pay outside in leather bags.'

*

The trees – like consonants about to proclaim and enwrap: bushes – the vowels that waver with the breath that wags the forest all together. Yes, yes, it is the sound, that gives the meaning, binds it all together in a story, sound of breath, of breeze, that sets it on a voyage, under sail, and tells me all I need to know, about the storms, the fires at sea, the havens – all going on when I'm no more. It tells me everything that is, and it is neither good nor bad, but it engrosses everything.

These heaps of automobiles – at first, they bother me, they're too disastered now to sleep in, all those prickly edges, springs and levers. I wish I had a servant, maybe several, to heave them out or bury them – those carcasses, those beasts, Impalas, Mustangs, Chargers, Mavericks, Pintos and Colts – and yet they've taken on the colour and the silence, the colour when it rains, silence in the minute before the wind catches and blows through – rustling out those journeys in the snow, making love in deserts. Leave them be, and don't be fussy. When the wind blows, you move with it. It's trees, descending and ascending, a text blown through – the birds aloft, no crows' nests here, held up by nothing, no song and twitter, just little commas and full stops, breasting, trailing in the wind.

It isn't here for anything: but over there, beyond the auto wrecks you can see the shelters, the guys, the families, that come to sleep: the shaky bothies, partly boughs and foliage, and partly canvas, oilskin, all improvised and in the day deserted. Not real nomads, these, just journeying, and refugees. Don't fuss, don't bother them. I watch, I'm not observed.

Sometimes, there's the sound of drums, coming from outside somewhere, a nuisance or a message, quite inscrutable. Then, a long time passes, maybe a week or more. The leather money-pouches are left, I bury them. A scroll that says, 'Don't forget the Power', along with banknotes, all stamped with 'Specimen', nowhere to spend, of course. There's people all around, though fleeting, yet some sleep here, leave their dreams, though I should not romanticise them: dreams are dreams, they come and go, they're just like you, you can't do much about them. That Power – some god, or someone's CIA? – an invitation, perhaps, to start my own, my agency, or if I'd done so, place mine obedient under theirs? – and I ignore it all.

The stuff here is so heavy, and so intricate – the trees – the proud ascenders, pine needles like the dust off type, the auto wrecks: a servant couldn't help me move it all around. I think to put up signs that say, 'Man Fridays, go away' – but it's unwelcoming, or even racist, or I might say instead 'no hands required', but that seems worse. Ah, Robinson! survivor of a massacre, alone with his God, and then the fantasy – the gay romance, the greatest – a black slave bonding, and in bondage.

Robinson! lover, father, brother – imagine them, the guys, hauling the excavators our hero salvaged from the wreck, digging for treasure ... Treasure Robinson knows – lies incarnate in the other ... And I want none of that, love that turns into its contrary. Love into exasperation – has put me where I am.

The food – is always here. I didn't need to kill the animals – just poking round, you find some store of little things, the food of wonderland – blinis, *pirozhky*, *dolmades*; and the streams – are Nebbiolo, Dolcetto. Use your brains, and you'll live well.

If I change my shape – it wouldn't show. There's no one here to watch. Not worth the doing, anyway – all here seems so purposeful, to look for more seems crass, it's all a presence: wind whistles round, streams run, moose hide, snow comes and goes, the rain...and so it carries on.

I don't forget the Power.

The forest, so they say, is home, to hermit and outlaw – the everyday is much the same for both.

Then, They – the Power – send a contract. For life, it says, protecting from the beasts and demons here. A shield from retribution.

I stand and watch the empty clearing, waiting for more beasts to come on stage. The people too, they come and flow, people pushed out and over, just on the move, from crimes that's done, to come, or just invented. I ask a woman where she's from.

'That's a funny question,' Mia says. 'Now I'm here, and what you really want to know is where I'm going, when I leave.'

'No,' I say, 'I really don't care. No one asks if those barge-haulers, in the picture, convicts, if they were innocent – they stand there, tensed forward, pictured for their representation. Nothing more. The millions in the camps – we don't grasp them, their everyday, it's "why" we ask. How is it possible? – and so and so.'

'No,' she says, 'I don't understand, this fixing on the blame, the judgement. We're here, and so are you, because it is a crossing-place. You're here to watch. And count,' and I interrupt, 'No one's crossing here!'

'Not yet,' she says. 'But everywhere one day becomes a frontier. And you're its guard.'

This is all new: I say, 'There's trees and beasts. That's all.'

'You should eat some. Show them who's boss,' she says.

I tell her, 'It's not about a hierarchy. True, they watch each other carefully, the beasts, the people, not to find a monarch, though – there's many skills, and no one's tops. Each wants their security, a day of calm, to bathe, to sing the song.'

'That may be wise,' Mia says. 'But wisdom's a bad guide. Remember what they call Dark Age – then, the wisest man on earth knew more than millions more. And now we have a store of facts and stuff that will outlast us all. We've never known so much, it will endure, it's like the pyramids – they last, a little chipped and shabby. That knowledge will endure when we have gone, gone down, the world as well, and no one left to rob our tombs, or dig a hole for anyone.'

We watch the treetops straining in the wind – oh to be off somewhere, and leave below the guys that lounge and want a place to sit.

'It's all excuses, anyway,' Mia says.

'Lots is,' I say. 'But what to do with what is inexcusable?'

'That sounds it's your problem. Keep off, you say, thin ice, deep slush here,' she says. And of course, I confess again, but make it sound positive, and full of doubt.

'I suppose we were married,' I say, 'At least, we had a party.'

'Everyone needs a party,' she says, 'to join, or get sick at. Perhaps you invited all the gods and nymphs as well,' and we kid along.

'Of course,' I say. 'They couldn't come, but metaphysics came and took a glass or two.'

She doesn't understand, it's not so hard. 'The lights, lights on the branches,' she says, 'and that leftover kind of food – the blinis. I love blinis – not the caviar, though,' and she turns her nose away.

'Here you can't have lights,' I say, 'we've no connection.'

'Like us,' she says, 'we're unconnected. And anyway, you don't get married in a forest, there's no one there to see. So there's no contract,' and I think of my thick unread bond, my contract, as if you need to set things down. Confess, don't tell the truth – good motto that.

'This here's an open community,' I say. 'The animals – they come, they move away, but always there's an order, or a search for it,' and she's impatient.

'This is a Crossing – for people, not for animals. You're not here to stop the crossing, just observe. We'll all be on the move as well, to seek the good life, I suppose.'

'It's not convincing,' I tell her. 'Your guys seem to fight a lot at night, the beasts are mostly quiet, those that have gotten through the day. But – it's a settlement.'

'It's so,' she says. 'At night, there is a lot of rivalry and sounding off. Not just beating on the weak, but challenging as well.'

'Who'll use the crossing, then?' I ask. 'You seem to know so much. Who'll cross from that to this, and seek for what?'

Mia doesn't answer, maybe doesn't know. It's not

to be reduced to elegance, this pattering of halfshod feet, it's in the books, cause and effect.

'This isn't even a frontier,' I say. 'Nor a faultline.'

She stares at me, and in a while she says, 'I guess it's always instinct, but we shall resist. We bastard mongrels, temporary residents and settlers here, we will resist.'

I say, 'I've no disrespect. How could I, anyway? I'm scum, as well you know.'

'Fuck your disrespect,' she says.

Should I run? Or seek protection from the law, its punishments and praise. We must love justice – so they say – but I don't want it done to me. Or should I stand and count the people – those at rest, like Mia here, and those still running, mouths open with no sound, fleeing from fire into new fires? Bearing totems disassembled, bits canvas-wrapped, or abandoned – it's all new, no one wrote down the history: 'Night in the Trojan horse', 'A deserter's tale – Thermopylae'. And yet – it's not beyond imagining. Running – like water, like ants whose hole's been blocked, a Disney forest fire, our past, our mothers, eaten up in orange scrawls.

I say aloud, 'Ours – an infancy without food.' Maybe that wedding food will stop, and then we eat the living, I suppose.

'Who knows,' she says. 'We – they, the settlers

here – may be better than you lot. Besides, what you did was stupid, screwing up your life – and on a whim.'

'Not noble, I agree. If she's dead, I'm free, and if she lives, condemned. Why not just renounce her? Let progress shuffle on, like it's supposed to. But – I don't have a "you lot" that I belong to.'

'Look in the glass,' she says, 'you'll find a million looking back.'

Maybe Mia, or they – running or settling – will be better. From fire to fire. And somehow break the chain.

'Well, Ranger,' she says, 'come and spend time with us. Sleep over. You do sleep? And when they complement my bum, just don't react – it's all part of the scene.'

'I sleep where I fall,' I say. 'Maybe that's what my lot does. I'll bring a pistol – physically, I'm a coward – so, if there's friction ...'

She's amused, pretends to be shocked: 'You can't mean to kill your hosts? Though you've had experience, as you're so keen to tell,' so, off we go, maybe this is a better lot than mine, perhaps the feet that swirl around our heads that night – maybe it's them, just passing through, that is the better lot. I feel I should stand up and count the gangs that pass, but like all guys in forward posts, I'm all a little country on its own, with just one citizen, no wish to communicate.

Indeed, the fear is thick, that if you speak you'll end up bad.

I tell Mia, 'You look quite like my wife – the hair, it's strawberry gold, although the words are finer than the stuff,' of course, she wishes she'd not heard, shrugs it all off. I wish that I'd not said, and maybe she is thinking she's in extra danger and I'm a loaded scatter-gun, and so I say, 'That dress, it's true, is tatty, almost medieval.'

'Well, as we're all kings and princesses here, and every night there's tourneys and some jousting – the kings with bottles, two-by-fours, the queens who scream and rush about, and pep the whole scene up – this little realm's beyond barbarian, but not a state, or nation, that's for sure.'

'That dress is quite a frock,' I say, those guys aren't hard, just lickered up, and Rangers don't seek power, and still less sex, they'd rather do philosophy and ride about, though in the forest riding isn't indicated, and nor is doing good or making Indians bow before the law, and so I sit and watch. Is this lot better than some other lots?

Mia says, 'You're so solemn – do things require it? You could try uncertainty with a smile.'

We watch a comic fight, two kings like circus clowns, they lash at each other – with laths, and over money, there's crying round like gulls. There's nothing to be said.

'What you want to do?' I ask. 'Bring peace?'

I start to see the colours – usually you watch the height of trees, but that's all monochrome, and just hot or cold, windy or still or wet, the bushes and the grass like crinkly sand.

I say, 'The animals don't see colours like we do – to them it's friendly wavelengths, or foes that break out, like discords or the TV going mad.'

'It's a circus where no one knows tricks,' I say.

She says, 'We stick together, for now.'

Mia has a feral look. I like that.

I say, 'You're almost noble, you know – on the edge, but managing. Till the centre goes down.'

'The centre's scum,' she says. 'All we get is insults and leftovers.'

I say, 'Have you seen the crowds in airports, where something unexplained has happened, they wheel and peak and drop like starlings. Run a little. Mutter. Not like a real parade, a procession like – "the tanks leave!" The victors strut along. Look at the colour, the flags, the armament! Kings and ostriches, drooping heads, the captives know their history ... and on it all unrolls. Where are they going? What honours avoiding, created? We can't ask them, we may never know. New deals are cooking, but we need the flourish – forward trumpeters! Some things do end, we clap and shout!'

'We don't,' she says.

'That's why they don't like you your lot. You don't volunteer. Don't join. Don't have another language, or religion. Just – seem to have something ... you don't go away: even when you're miserable, you don't eat all the animals, cut down all the trees and sell them ...'

'It's not a quality,' she says. 'It's just we don't have saws. But it's true, we think we are the same as all the rest, but then our difference shakes them up. We ought to go, we don't. As savages, we should be happy. And the guys, the modern city guys – in the end, they'll run. They'll have to, and of course, we'll let them through. And then? Where do we go? What do we eat?'

'Hmmm,' I say. 'It's a puzzle that sex and love and rituals, and drugs and opera, can't help to solve. Those lovely banknotes, big as a rug, with violet and mulberry scrolls – the bank is far away, if it still works – and here there's nothing you can buy, except each other.'

'Well, we've settled that – for you and me. Nothing. No relationship!' says Mia. 'What luck! What destiny.'

We contemplate ourselves. Then I say, 'Of course, the world wouldn't all fall down at once. Not everybody runs at first. Someone somewhere wouldn't let it happen. Interests, you know ...'

'But lots of guys will have to run, to walk, to

limp, through here,' she says.

I say, 'Hurrah for Russians, and their finger food! Let weddings turn them on – blinis, *pirozhky* – and when divorces turn them off, we'll party more! It's their great gift ...' but she is not so sure.

'I fear,' she says. 'We are the ones that's scrutinised! Forget the Russians and free food – it's us, in the clearing here, and you (who knows what you're for) they have in mind to be a model for a settlement. If we survive, we'll be a cluster – ones who know how they can scrape along, and interrupt their trek and shelter in some forest clearing – while others run on by and end up nowhere.'

I'm quite confused and ask, 'Who's looking, then? Russians or Americans, or is it Romans we are at?' and Mia says, no, it's civilisation some powerful guys are looking at, to see if it hangs on, and how, when everything else has fallen down.

She says, 'It's here that civilisation ends, or starts, or just runs on. We haven't built or etched or hammered – just stood here, some confident, most scared. Mortality will give us shape, mistakes repaired by grave-time, projects go forward by the inch, and mostly here we stand, and chat or float along in melancholy ...'

I say, 'Why not, Mia? Yours is as good a group as you can find. We'll never lack, so long as those *pirozhky* are available – so, off you'll go each day to do your trade, whatever that may be, and then come home to fight and drink – and you will be the nucleus! Yes, carry the species forward, breed we must – from rarity to bold excess, and start it over, all again. It's life without the sentimental – I'm your man! And you are you,' and I'm quite proud of Mia, standing there, a draggle-tail of dress, and bare but pretty feet.

She says, 'How do you know all that?'

I say, 'It must be so, if not, there isn't any hope.'

There's a jangling and a rumble. I'm sure it is my wife, climbing from the hole, with demons; like original sin. No.

It's a convoy of little carts, the horses splaying out their legs, low carriages that find a hidden pathway through the trees. The drivers raise their trilbies as they pass – our Captain, Harbin, one of the leaders of our band, shouts 'Fuck off Gippoes' as they pass. They don't seem to want to stop. Our Captain says, 'No sound, no language we can understand,' and he must mean they've no boom box – nor do we, we've no power ... and on the convoy goes. I hear the Captain shout, 'Thieves, beggars, indigents,' and back there comes, 'Cheats and speculators: plastic gnomes,' and so our cultures clash, then all is quiet again.

The Captain says, 'Get rid of them! It is God's word, just like exterminations and the plagues,' but I am off to do my Ranger's job: and here's a guy, he's all alone.

'Hey there!' he says. 'You guys look pretty desperate, you haven't got much here,' and so we talk, it seems the city's been deserted, there being neither food nor power.

He laughs, and says, 'I lived in Central Avenue, wow, did that all fall down!'

He makes a sign that says, 'It's flattened', and I say, 'I loved the scene, the bars, the sex, the pills, the booze – life rising through the cracks, like sycamores that thrust up through the sidewalks ...'

I go on, until he says, 'The thing is was – why'd you buy 'napartment if all you wanted was strolling up the Street?' and he's not wrong, though all is lost, and so one dream flows like a stream into another – that I'm here in uniform, and real and waiting.

'If I were you, my friend,' I say, 'I'd move along, there's nothing here and we're defending it,' and wonder why I don't take my own advice.

He says, 'You guys – just squatting here, beneath the trees: you'll never build a church, a house, a mosque. You're pretty flat—'

'We each one has his style of life and aspirations,' I interrupt. 'Everyone is on the move, is driven by disaster or by greed, but deep inside we have our stories and our hopes, they're like a frieze of angels in our heads—'

'And much good may it do you,' and he's off, but it is good to have some news and know the worst has happened, not to you.

'Ranger,' Mia says, 'you're not sexy, but you are bizarre,' and she chuckles approvingly.

Mia's singing. Just voice. And shouting, rattling with the bottom of her throat. All the sounds she has inside. Not like a bird with its script.

'You haven't got a key,' I say.

'I haven't got a door to put it in,' she says.

'You don't use language.'

'We don't use much here,' she replies quickly, 'and only curses and questions.'

'Is this starting things or finishing, do you think?' I ask.

It's a wrong question. Starting or finishing. That's something the world does, not what Mia does.

All the leaves have fallen off the trees. Are they starting or finishing? It's like the guy here, Frank, who does little paintings, that don't refer to anything. Yet – they're paintings. That don't refer to anything.

We're quite the creative colony, here, just we can't build a shelter – but what is coming? Shelter from what? The fire, the rain, the air, the water, a falling tree?

Another guy, here, looks like a plasterer. 'Ivan the Ranger,' he says. 'Hmm. Could have a war record with that name.'

'I've got a record.' I say. 'It keeps going round and round! No, I've just made the one casualty, and that was probably an error in the counting.'

'There's lots of couples splitting with the stress,' he says. 'The ladies set up stalls and sell their partners' things.'

'Did you see a bruised one?' I ask. 'Selling books in Cyrillic, Arab writing, stuff like that?'

'Sure!' he says. 'You were the booky kind?'

I don't know if he's truthful. If she lives, there's trouble waiting down the line.

'I like the squiggles,' I say, offhand, 'nothing more – as if your eyesight's in a spin.'

He shambles off; these guys – they're full of hope: off up the slope and in the sun, and leave us here...

Mia says, 'I guess the Captain, Harbin's winning all the fights. He'll be the boss, the lord we're now to call him, and he'll set some marks and that will be his land, and he should be the one we pay, he'll send us off to war and jail us too, if he decides. But there'll be peace, decisions too – he'll make them all, without a wait.'

I say, 'You'll dig for him, and for yourselves. It all sounds pretty trite. You'll have to chop the trees, if you grow beans. Then there's the question of the animals, and all the finger food – who's to get that? In any case, I am a Ranger, so I don't respect these rules, these boundaries—'

'While you live here,' she interrupts, 'you don't have much choice,' and she is right, though while I'm here I'm free from retribution, like a bird.

'Well,' I say, 'I guess all that fraught and fight was showing Captain Harbin is the strongest. And he's found himself a chair.'

Indeed he has. He sits and hands out justice. I'm pleased I don't need any.

'He wants us all to work,' says Mia. 'Planting stuff. And digging lots, I guess.'

'It's as I said,' I tell her, and I think – how to get out of work here? – doing nothing, being a soldier idle but on call.

'I'm a Ranger with a uniform,' I say. 'But I still don't want to join the bunch that's throwing up a rampart. Tell me what's to do.'

Mia says, 'You need a skill. It seems free food is coming to an end. What can you tell, what can you remember, of the orderly life?'

I think hard. A century of references has slipped, it hasn't left a shred, and we've no power, no power to bring it back. What memories, what civilisation? I say,

'There was my father's favourites. Pauline Julien for one. Glière. There must be more. The painters –

well, no point in that, we haven't got a wall to put
them on. The poets now – I found a book of stuff –
Jehan Rictus, maybe he is new to you?'

She looks disappointed. 'That's all you
remember? It wouldn't take too long to spread your
memories around,' and I'm annoyed.

'No, no.' I say. 'I don't want to stay around and
watch that Captain Harbin lord it like a cock, and beat
us up, and him all growing old and past it – still feisty,
and aggressive still, and march us off to war – no, I
don't want to see it all. I have a bigger boss, and
comrades too, just waiting for the word to count the
people coming through ...'

This morning early, came a flight of nuns. And
later, bunches of guys on sticks, they must have
cleared the hospice out.

'Mia,' I say, 'if I stay, ours could be the greatest
love story of all time, though neither wants the other –
and it could be better still, if I went away. A love that
isn't consummated always wrings a tear in folk that's
sensitive; or maybe just one night, and then castration,
or some noble quest ...'

She laughs, and says I'd better go – but surely
everywhere there's captains this and that, quite likely
all around, and ramparts, judgement seats and oaths
and faiths, and buildings of all sorts, and jails. I say
again, 'No, no, I don't want to wait around and see it
all.' I stamp my foot, like Alice, on the forest floor. It

doesn't yield, no magic rabbits take my hand.

I think, 'Fuck it! Just a Ranger, Ranger Ivan – but I won't plant and dig. I'll find some way!'

I say, 'If my bosses can't protect me, I must find something to save me from the digging. I thought perhaps – football coach?'

She laughs, 'All the football jobs are long gone – even the kicking part.'

'Well,' I say. 'If, as they tell me now, the universe was made by chance – maybe the same chance may end the whole display tomorrow.'

'Some chance,' she says. 'You a bookie?'

'I thought – philosopher.'

'Try for court jester,' she says.

'Maybe a bishopric. A prophet's tree, perhaps, would suit.'

I've lost hope. My bosses need to rescue me.

Mia says, 'Harbin wants to sell – just the best of us. Not to go begging. Getting rid of.'

I say, 'He can't sell me – I've got a bigger boss – that CIA guy, if he reappears. They've got a global scan, they work the future out. A sale would be void.'

She's not impressed. The digging wears her down.

I say, 'They throw a line, that over days and even years, relationships develop. Then you can use them – they sort things out, it seems.'

She says, 'I thought your option was castration.'

'That promises a little for a little,' I say. 'Let's go on to think how our love might tie us in to something good.'

We both think back. Lovers grow close by doing things alongside – they call it sharing, though it's hard to see what's shared, except some time, and that goes on regardless. As we've no power, the TV, movies, car and music – they're all out. For housework, you need houses. Philosophy, maybe ...

She says, 'That thing about the universe – it wasn't chance, but law!'

I'm irritated, and I say, 'You think that chance is lawless? Ask a jockey! Rules are rules, the dice, the cards, obey. The causal chain, my dear...' We think that through, and then I say, 'Let's not discuss – you know how talking riles me up,' and I am sure we both think of my wife, her snitty talk, and how our silences were good, although it's hard remembering a silence – silence counts when someone's caught wordless in a conversation or debate.

'This love,' Mia says. 'It seems it's all a chemistry, that makes you overlook the points in which you both are weak. I'll ask the guys, as they go running through ...'

I say, 'You mean, you'll get some dope? To make us fall in love? An epic passion? Mia, that is genius, but I have a fear – no one is selling – and we have no cash.'

We fall to silence, silence I'll remember all my life.

Of course – there's cash. I buried lots beneath that tree.

'Harbin says he'll get power put on,' Mia says, 'That way we can catch up.'

'Appliances?' I ask. 'The guys we see are mostly carrying toasters – you'll not get much news from them.'

'Well,' she says, 'You're no hotter on history than you were on culture. Toasters is civil life.'

It's maybe so. It's all a mishmash. Time's been curried – it's all hot and secret, but doesn't seem to mean so much.

Mia says, 'They say the deaths – out there – are awful.'

That will be true. Harbin must have the bigger picture – so he says – but who is after who, it's hard to say. Evil is all around, and lashing out: and so is fear – it's in the air, like rooks ... Up there in the trees, their fuzzy castles – maybe I could perch up there, that way you get a bigger picture too. And safe, unless there's wind. Or fire.

'Don't fret,' says Mia. 'The CIA will come for

you. At least you needn't dig.'

I say, 'Those river pirates – took us by surprise. And Harbin's built the rampart with their cadavers sprouting out.'

The agents, CIA, arrive. They're dressed as hunters, though there's nothing here to shoot but us.

My guy says, 'Now it's back to normal, though your city's trashed. We'll do you all a favour. Those trees maybe could fetch a price. And Captain Harbin – of the worst, he is the best – he's got you all a-scurrying and a-digging.'

Power will come back, and with it, luxury, and we shall see the other guys in other parts, how they can dig and scurry, and what bad wave is coming next!

My guy goes on, 'Now that the Time of Running's done, you must all stay still. You're settled here, and I've some passports making sure you don't run round some more.'

I say, 'I'm a Ranger, so I don't need ...' but he gives me one.

I say, 'That isn't me. That religion isn't mine.'

He says, 'If it's a religion of the faith, then you can lie. Religions of the truth – well, if they catch you with detectors, then it's thinking fast you need.'

'Well, where's we go?' I ask.

'To walk along the Street,' Mia says, 'that pub that's painted pink, the mortadella in the stores, the clothes that aren't just frocks.'

'Yes,' I think, 'the sages too, and alphabets, and movies,' and there is great nostalgia for the good, the better, life.

The agent says, 'If Harbin says you go, you go. and then come back. You didn't count the guys all rushing through – so, we could leave you dangling here, but – our investment must be saved ...' and I wonder what is payback, when's the time.

'Decide!' says Mia. 'Stay or escape. The wood. The Street.'

'I decide for me,' I say. 'I can't engage with you. Besides – I can take a leap, but not give shape to what comes after.'

'I want a deed!' says Mia. 'There's not been many words, it's true – but "Jump or Slump" I say.'

'Oh, I'll leap down,' I say. But lovers' leaps are not for me – they go on going down.

'They won't let you leave,' says Mia. 'You'll stay, standing for something. And it's not so bad. The world, it crackled up, but now it's better. Harbin has a dress consultant.'

'It's the city,' I say. 'I miss it, more than people.'

'What does it matter?' she asks. 'It seems to me – your memory's been rooted in a cluster of streets, some friends, and some forgotten: music. Just little things. Your city's made of rats' nests, little tangles.'

I say, 'Maybe – though it lets me talk to millions. Invisible, it's true. What do you expect from memory?

Class, nation, faith? You have to find the factor that is right for you – it's been like this for years and years.'

She nods: 'Well, that's what lets you live here, in this wood.'

'If it's all a tragedy,' she says later, 'before it all plays out, there must be hope. And if there's hope, there's respect too – at least for some. When there's tragedy to come.'

Habin is doing well. His circle spreads. Few soldiers, and more tarts. Marines – up and down the river – even more clumps of trees, more guys who dig, and dig for him, and solemn guys who wear clean shirts, and come to call and do some deals. Even cars to park.

I say to Mia, 'It's a video game – they don't know if they're in it or are playing.'

'You should try the jobs where you don't dig and hack,' she says.

'But I'm a Ranger—' I start to say but she interrupts, she's looked me up.

'Rangers? Thousands of them. I think I found you, you're the one – warehousing, packaging, driving high-class vans. Setting up marquees – that must be you. Curriculum.'

I say, 'The world of stuff, and buying things – that's my specialty. I know it thoroughly. It gives you time to do philosophy.' I laugh to show I wasn't always dumb. Time there once was, and not bunched up like it is here.

'I dislike the colour of her hair,' Harbin says, pointing at Mia. 'Doesn't seem quite natural. So – off she goes with you!'

Usually, these bossy guys like lots of light and mirrors – so's they can see themselves, and also who is doing who behind your back. Instead, he perches in a grotto, there's a movie crew around – not a decent one, with railroad tracks and names on chairs, just teenagers: the principle's the same.

'We dug your pouches up,' he says. 'And hold the cash in – in escrow! – or ransom. That way you'll both be back.'

He pours Mia and me each a tumbler of brandy. 'That,' he says, 'is the stuff you'll run the boat on! Up and down the river. You will make a map, of all those little kingdoms, up and down, and river pirates too – I have a mind to build ...'

He talks for an hour about the project. He needs that map, we'll be unarmed, – the marines have been no good, except at firing at the shore. A river empire. First, a federation of all the other bosses, doing down the pirates, then you do down the bosses too, off with their heads, that stuff.

He ends, 'The empires based on land and sea – they all have failed. I'll try one with a river as its base, its artery! So – off you float, and map the future. By the way – you needn't think to run away. Some guys have seen your pad,' he laughs at me. 'First, it was trashed, then it fell in on itself – pressed cardboard, so it seems – those walls. The ceiling's stuck down to the floor.'

As we leave, Harbin says, 'You must have hope. Hope is a whore – anyone can have her!' and he laughs again.

'He's got a book full of sayings,' says Mia, hustling me along.

'You seem to know a lot about him,' I say, glad to be leaving.

We're on the shore. There's bottles here, and mud – degraded weapons of all sorts, and guys that walk around not doing much. It is a sign of power, all right: and here's a jerrycan of brandy, here's the boat – is that supposed to be a motor? – the cabin's fallen in on itself, it's just a skiff with logs and blackened stuff on top.

I say, 'We're like the owl and the pussycat,' and she says,

'I bet you put yourself down as the bird of wisdom.'

I say, 'Do we lie down in this thing, or sit up? If we lie down, they'll think it's empty and steal it. If we sit up, they'll shoot at us.'

'We could sing,' Mia says. 'That's a kind of compromise.'

'Whose guitar did they dance to? Quite civilised

that pair, only dancing to accompaniment,' I say. Mia says, 'Well, it was a wedding, like the Russians have. I remember how there was singing and dancing. Poetry too, all the trip along. And vows.'

I say, 'Perhaps everyone then had music training. Who played – the pig or the turkey?'

We don't remember. 'I'm hungry,' I say.

I tell Mia, 'Go and beg for food. No sex, it takes you too long.'

We've been paddling with the current. I say, 'How'll we get back? We've drunk most of the fuel.'

The settlements along the banks: – some guys with poles are fishing. Some villages are full of shouting, some seem to be on fire. Mostly there's huts among the bushes. Hard to tell if we are floating into light from dark, or the other way around – there's variety.

'Who ever would want to make an empire out of these poor guys?' I say.

Some have put up shrines. I guess they are devout.

Mia says, 'Harbin wants more soldiers – and besides, think of the future. You can screw stuff out these places when they get started up.'

She adds, 'Our trees are sold.'

I say, 'Rowing must have been difficult – that cat and the owl.'

'Sex too,' says Mia.

'At least they had a decent boat,' I say.

Mia says, 'If you don't make it back, then the cash is mine. I need it to become a courtier.'

'A handmaiden,' I say. 'And I wonder what that might involve! Maybe I'll be off. Winter is coming.'

'None of us will leave,' she says. 'Unless we're sold. And Rangers can't be sold.'

Mia says, 'Harbin's a fighter. Not like those other guys – that one that paid for sex and boasted. That other, for ever marrying celebs. Another one – the saint who made those wars! Harbin is tough.'

I say, 'He's a bully. Where's he want to take us, take you all? And if I follow him – I've betrayed. Lost my Ranger badge.' We both laugh.

Mia says, 'Luxuria. That's the word that brought us down. Then running. And saying we're were rich and randy.'

It's not for me to make a comment. We float on down. Here there are huts, some palisades. Those must be the fever trees – we shiver when we see them. Mia goes ashore to beg our food – it's mostly beans. And eggs. Some guys have found the flats where salt accumulates, and Mia says that if there isn't gold, salt's what the Captain wants. And guys are making charcoal, gathering clay, and digging down for speculation – and I write it down.

This village sees a future – here's some guys, they've gone from whittling to making tables, there's a sign, it says 'Festa della zuffa'. Mia asks, 'A *zuffa*, what's that? Edible?'

I tell her, there's a big party and it ends in fights, just like real parties do, but this one, after the general scrum, it ends in peace between the villages. She casts a cold eye.

There's bigger, heavier birds round – they must be from the sea. And now, the mangroves end. It is the sea. The sea, the sea!

So we embrace, and weep, and there it lies, a bigger and a calmer thing than we have seen before. No people, that's a blessing, just ticking over, waves regulated, colours programmed, I suppose, a bit monotonous, and sure – to venture on it would be foolish – but, after all, the Sea, the Sea!

'Why're we so excited?' Mia asks, and I say, 'Maybe it's a thing without a limit, and indifferent,' and Mia says, 'I'm sure it is, all that.'

Mostly guys just stare at us, but here's some friendly ones. 'They're too nice here,' she says, we reckon they are looking for some human sacrifice. We hurry on.

'No heads on poles,' she laughs. 'They're waving us goodbye.'

Then, there's disaster – we're paddling back, upstream and going slow. And here's the river pirates – this big guy, he's on me, and he's holding, hitting, panting worse than me, I shout,

'What the fuck you looking for? All we got is what you see,' but he won't quit, there's something bright and keen that's dancing round my body, and I see poor Mia, in a mess, and all confused, and doesn't know where she should pitch her voice, to call or send it down inside – what words might be of use.

We've nothing, and they leave us, I tell Mia that we're lucky, but we don't believe it,

'They cut my hand right off,' I say.

'You're right!' Mia says, 'there's nothing there. That was a kind of wanton thing,' and I agree.

She says, 'Wrap up what isn't there – here's some big leaves.'

I say, 'Some magic there? A healing plant, perhaps?'

'No, no,' she says. 'You're dripping on my clothes,' but all the same, it soon heals up – what isn't there – and in another clump of huts a whittler's found who makes me an oak claw, and ties it on.

'These should click open, friend,' I say, but, no, it's just a claw.

'It looks distinguished,' Mia says, 'just it's not tied on to your brain.'

The guy's so proud, the first he's ever made, and

so claw grasps the paddle, and we're off again. I think it spoils the Ranger look, but Mia says to lose a hand is quite a gain, for you can't dig, and you can use the other one for giving orders....

'We shan't tell Harbin all the bad things we have seen,' she says. 'Maybe some guys are killed and eaten, some just killed – religion is religion, war is war, we shouldn't judge or make hypotheses,' and that is right, and I'll just count the households, if that is what they are, – or just the number of the huts, and if there's long or tall ones, and she says, 'After all, the darkness we bring with us.'

'That's quite some platitude,' I say, and she laughs and says they're what the world is made of, otherwise we'd not know where we lived. And we are quite good friends, despite not liking anything at all too much, the situation being dour, and death is in those boats that keep on skimming out – though seeing that we've nothing, and that Mia's in a mess – I shoo them off A waving of my claw's the sign, call it surrender or some voodoo, the effect is just the same.

'I love you, Mia,' I say.

'Paddle harder.'

I say, 'My arms is numb.'

'Wait,' she says. 'I'll nail your claw to the wood, the paddle. It's just a symbol after all.'

'What's the hurry?' I ask.

'Harbin's a great man, just like I said. He needs

his map. And you were sweet, you almost saved me. The screaming was fantastic.'

I ask, 'Why're you so keen on that bully Harbin? Just to be his handmaiden, maybe I could be his handyman, ha ha,' but she is not amused.

'That's what he promised,' she says. 'No digging.'

I'm unmoved. 'I've cooked myself with the CIA. And with you. Who wants a Lonely Ranger?' but she's not moved.

'The CIA will do a deal with Harbin,' she says. 'They like little empires that drill for oil and diamonds.'

The settlements pass slowly by. Flags. Some red, some black, and some with skulls and crossbones too.

I say, 'I prefer the villages that follow Islam. 'Peace' is a less unlikely thing than 'love', the Christian pitch. Love is a hit-and-miss, but peace can always be negotiated. Then there's the realists, they pray to all the threats, the spirits, though that avails them least. Maybe so, they worry less,' and I go on and on, but Mia's anxious to be back, and when we see a tuft of trees, she's overboard and swimming on, her dress splays out behind, a frill, bell of a medusa, maybe, and then she's gone. I say aloud,

'Oh no, another woman disappeared, another limb gone missing – even though they're nothing but some symbols, they make you go to jail, or on the block,'

but then I think, of course, here there's useful trees to
hang a guy, to spare the cleaning of a block.

Here's Harbin, and he says, 'Disappeared? Mia? Hope
lost. But not abandoned – that's a step up, more
dignified.' He laughs. His shirt is clean. The movie
crew is big, they powder him, some guy has wired the
Captain's ears, and everyone he wants is listened to.

'Give me your hand!' he says, 'Or rather not!'
and laughs. 'Well, that is life! Woman gone, hand too!
Boy! is that life?!' he laughs some more, the other
guys laugh too, but silently.

'OK, now let's see your map,' he says. 'Those
pirates didn't get that too?'

'Why would they want a map?' I ask. 'They want
to keep away from maps!'

'Hmmmm. Ho. Hum,' he says, peering at the
sheet. 'Less people round, so there'll be less clearing
up to do. I bet life will go on another hundred years or
more, after all that nonsense, that disaster. Everything
burnt up. Thinned us out. Pity about your apartment,
but here we are. I did all right, and you and Mia
almost managed it,' and then I see her – reappeared,
remade. Her hair is dyed, like Russians have, she's
wearing shorts truncated– she is transformed.

'I'm a handmaiden,' she crows, seizing my claw
and clowning, waving it aloft for all.

'What the fuck you mean?' asks Harbin angrily.

'Just fooling, Master. Some punning fun, that's
all. The Ranger's just a friend.'

Harbin turns back to the map and says, 'Those
guys are planting lots of beans – they blow you out,
but here there's clay, and there's a hole that's full of
who knows what – and there's some priests, and lots
of guys that's longing to be soldiery.'

And on he goes, the guys all cluster round and
talk of war and peace.

Those seabirds, heavy with the will to find the sea
again – their place; horizon receding to infinity, no
compromise, the colours changing automatically, from
grey to blue to green. Calling to no one with their
lonely cries – and how I envy them, those birds
without a land.

About the author

John Fraser has lived in Rome since 1980. Previously,
he worked in England and Canada.